Melanie

Finding Mr Right

Welcome to the first book in Leigh Michaels's wonderful new trilogy—all about dating games and the single woman!

Meet **Kit, Susannah** and **Alison**. Three very special women who are friends, business partners—and happily single! Ambitious and successful, they live life to the fullest and have no room on their agenda for husband hunting!

But it seems they don't have to go looking for Mr Right…because each finds themselves unexpectedly pursued by their very own dream date….

First, we see Kit, sensitive and practical, organizing a bachelor auction that brings an exciting surprise when she wins **The Billionaire Date**.

Bubbly and impulsive Susannah thought she'd never see Marcus again after their affair ended—until a work project brings them together and Susannah faces **The Playboy Assignment** (April #3500).

And warmhearted Alison can no longer deny her craving for a baby when she meets a doctor who could help her, and finds herself taking on **The Husband Project** (May #3504).

You'll laugh, you'll cry, but you won't be able to put these books down as you share in a very special friendship between three wonderful women, and fall in love with the gorgeous men who—eventually— win them over!

Dear Reader,

Over the years I've greatly enjoyed writing books that are connected—sequels, prequels and spin-offs. They usually come about because a secondary character in one book is so interesting that he or she demands a story of their own. But until now I've never tackled an interconnected set of books, knowing from the very beginning that the stories would be so closely tied together that—while each book can stand alone—the three form a very special package. So the **Finding Mr Right** trilogy has been both a challenge and a joy.

My editor and I had been talking about a trilogy for some time, and I'd been looking for the perfect setting in which my heroines could be business partners as well as friends. Then one of my friends mentioned that her sister was a partner in an all-woman public relations firm in Kansas City, Missouri. Now that was a story possibility made just for me, since I have a journalism background and public relations experience. And though, to this day, I know nothing more about that real-life PR firm than that it employs only women, I want to thank the members of that company for the inspiration they provided for the **Finding Mr Right** trilogy.

And I thank you, my wonderful readers, for following along through the fifteen years since my first book was published, all the way to this new challenge. I think you'll enjoy meeting Kit, Susannah and Alison every bit as much as I enjoyed writing about them. I must warn you, though—I cried when I had to give up these three special new friends....

With love,

P.S. I love to hear from readers! You can write to me at: P.O. Box 935, Ottumwa, Iowa, 52501-0935.

Leigh Michaels

The Billionaire Date

Harlequin Books

TORONTO • NEW YORK • LONDON
AMSTERDAM • PARIS • SYDNEY • HAMBURG
STOCKHOLM • ATHENS • TOKYO • MILAN
MADRID • WARSAW • BUDAPEST • AUCKLAND

RECYCLED PAPER
RECYCLED PAPER

ISBN 0-373-03496-2

THE BILLIONAIRE DATE

First North American Publication 1998.

CHAPTER ONE

No MATTER how carefully she counted, Kit couldn't get past ten.

Of course, she told herself, the problem this time wasn't that she was mathematically inept—though she *was*, as a matter of fact, and her partners never hesitated to remind her of it. But she hadn't forgotten how to count. It was just that the room was small and crammed with giggling, nervous, very young women. Twelve of them, Kit knew. There had to be twelve. Except they were milling about, half-dressed, with makeup and hairbrushes and curling irons in hand, and no matter how carefully she tried to keep track of who was where, she could only see ten.

She climbed onto a chair and stuck two fingers in her mouth to give a keening whistle worthy of a professional sports referee. The sound level diminished instantly, and Kit took advantage of the opportunity. "Would everybody just shut up and stand still for one minute while I take roll?"

She counted heads. There were still only ten.

That figured, she thought. Just fifteen minutes before the start of the fashion show, with the audience already in place, two of her amateur models must have ducked off to the ladies' room. She only hoped they weren't actually sick with nerves.

Though it wouldn't be any surprise, considering the way the rest of the function's gone, she reminded herself. *At least it'll be over in two more hours, and with any luck I'll never have to deal with another fashion show*

5

in my life, or the debutante crowd, either. "Who's missing?"

The girls looked around as if surprised. Finally a slender blonde in the corner said, "Marliss and Shelby."

"Well, go find them, will you, Heather? We only have a few more minutes to get you all ready to go out on the runway."

Heather giggled. "I wish I *could.* Shelby's dad invited her to New York City for the weekend, and she asked Marliss to go with her. They're planning to see a Broadway show, and shop all the way across Manhattan, and—"

Kit's heart seemed to bounce off her toes. "They just took off for New York?"

"Well, sure," Heather said. "Wouldn't you, if you'd had the chance?"

In a flash, Kit wanted to say. *Or anywhere else, as a matter of fact.* "All right. Each of them was supposed to model three outfits, so somebody will have to double up." She reached for the clipboard that held the list of dresses and models arranged in sequence. "Jackie, you're first. If we can add another change in between your first two—"

The small, plump brunette shook her head. "I wouldn't mind, but I can't fit in the outfits they were going to model. That long gown Shelby looks so good in would drag clear to Kansas if I tried to wear it."

She was correct, Kit realized. "All right, who's the closest in size? I'll probably have to rearrange the order you go out in to leave time for the extra clothing changes." But she couldn't, she realized. Not only would the emcee be expecting them to follow the original schedule, but Kit had spent hours matching his cue cards to her list. She looked at the schedule and reminded herself that throwing the clipboard would do no good—even if it might make her feel better for a moment or two. "Who's closest in size?" she repeated.

The girls looked doubtfully at each other. "Well, actually, you are, Ms. Deevers," Jackie said finally. "Shelby's the tallest of us all, just about your height. And Marliss is skinny and flat-chested, just like you."

Thanks for pointing it out, Kit wanted to say. But sarcasm would do no good at the moment, and Jackie's observation was every bit as true as it was unflattering. For the thousandth time, Kit cursed the fashion show, the debs who had come up with the original idea and the mad impulse that had made her agree to bail them out after they'd gotten in over their heads. It had all looked so simple when they'd come into Tryad's office just two weeks ago, in despair over a fund-raising idea gone sour and in need of professional help.

"Sorry," Jackie added. "I didn't mean that the way it sounded."

"Never mind," Kit muttered. She took a deep breath. She was in for it, that was obvious. It was far too late to wash her hands of the mess and walk out. She'd have to follow through to the end. "All right—you'll have to get yourselves lined up for the first trip down the runway while I get dressed." She ran her gaze over the schedule and flipped through the clothing rack till she found Marliss's first outfit. Just an hour ago the garments had been arranged carefully in order of use. Then the girls had come in and started stirring things around as they got ready.

This bunch doesn't need a public relations person keeping them in line, she thought. *They need a lion tamer.*

She slid into a pair of sapphire blue chiffon harem pants. Despite their fullness, she felt as if she was wearing nothing at all. The fabric was so wispy it was translucent, and the band that held the garment up came to rest much closer to the curve of her hip than to her waist.

She wondered again, as she had earlier when she'd gotten her first good look at the racks, who had been such an idiot as to select these clothes to be modeled by girls still in their teens. But it was far too late for that question.

Kit was just reaching for the brief-cut top that matched the harem pants when the door opened.

"Who's in charge here?" a male voice demanded.

Hastily Kit pulled the top over her head, trying to look over her shoulder at the same time in order to get a glimpse of the owner of that rich, insistent voice. One of the girls' fathers, perhaps, objecting to her activities?

Well, if he was going to try to snatch his daughter out of the lineup at this late date, Kit decided, she'd... She'd make him take the girl's place and model her outfits himself!

The room had gone dead quiet.

Kit turned to face the intruder, still trying to settle her brief top into place. Her first impression was of height, dark good looks and a tuxedo that looked as if it had been molded to fit his frame. Then the aura of power that surrounded him hit her like the shock wave of an explosion, almost rocking her off her feet.

No wonder the girls went quiet, Kit thought wryly. She was ten years older than any of them and had a whole lot more experience with men. Still, the way this man was staring at her was enough to rob her of the ability to breathe. There was something about the expression in those huge, dark brown eyes....

Kit stepped forward and held out her hand. "You must be Jarrett Webster. I'm sorry I haven't had a chance to thank you for emceeing this event—"

His brows drew together. "I assume you're in charge?" He ignored her outstretched hand.

"I'm Kit Deevers, from Tryad Public Relations, and I'm coordinating the event, yes."

"Well, if you don't get this show on the road, not thanking me won't be the only thing you'll have to feel sorry about. I'll give you one more minute and then I'm going to start reading cue cards whether you have a model on the runway or not." He turned on his heel and strode out.

That, Kit fumed, *is the best example of arrogant high-handedness I've ever seen!* Didn't the man realize that amateur events hit snags sometimes? "All right, girls, you've got your marching orders. As soon as the music starts—"

"Uh, Ms. Deevers?"

Kit closed her eyes in pain. "What is it now, Jackie?"

"I just thought you should know before you go out in the auditorium. You've got that top on wrong."

Kit glanced down and swore.

Like the harem pants, the matching top contained just enough lining fabric to be decent, which meant that the front of the sapphire blue chiffon bodice was lined, but the back was not.

And in her haste to get covered up before turning to face a male intruder, she'd put the thing on backward.

Now she knew what Jarrett Webster's expression had been as he'd stood in the doorway and stared at her. It was incredulity. He hadn't been able to believe his eyes.

The show was over, and nobody had fallen off the runway. Nobody, in fact, had even broken a fingernail. Miracles did happen, Kit told herself. It was over—and she had survived. In another half hour or so, the follow-up reception would be finished, as well, and she'd be done with the whole mess.

Still wearing the last outfit she'd modeled, the long and slinky black silk gown that Shelby had been scheduled to show, Kit leaned against the shadowed side of a pillar in the reception hall and tried to become invisible. The marble pillar was comfortingly cool against her almost-bare back. Only a few narrow strips of satin ribbon separated stone from skin.

At least, she thought, there hadn't been any doubt about which direction to put on this particular outfit. Still, she could hardly wait to get out of it. Shelby, even at seventeen, was far better endowed than Kit was, and the girls had ended up stuffing tissue paper into the front of the dress to fill it out properly. The result was eye-catching but hardly comfortable.

Guests were starting to drift out of the reception hall, and nobody was paying any attention to Kit. She cast one final look around the room to be certain none of her models were doing anything to damage their borrowed finery. Perhaps she could make it to the dressing room. If she hugged the edge of the reception hall maybe no one would see and stop her. One well-meaning phrase of congratulation on the fashion show's success might be enough to send her over the edge into hysterical laughter.

But before she could move, a feminine voice from the far side of the pillar said, "I couldn't believe what I was seeing! Pushing herself in like that, in the midst of what should have been the girls' day." There was a strident undertone that belied the woman's soft drawl. "She modeled more than anybody else, for heaven's sake. One would have thought it was her own private fashion show—which is not at all what we hired her to do."

Kit bit her tongue and reminded herself that listening

to other people's conversations was guaranteed to bring unpleasant sensations to the eavesdropper. *And after all,* she thought, *it's done now. That's the important thing.*

"I wondered why you hired her at all, Colette."

Kit shrank closer against the pillar and sneaked a look over her shoulder. Not that she needed to. She'd have recognized that rich, intense voice across the vastness of outer space. There was a frosting of arrogance that she'd bet never quite vanished.

"Oh, Jarrett, darling, you know one never quite has time to manage everything. I must say, however, we all thought when we hired her that we were going to get *professional* assistance."

Kit could see only the woman's back. The rest of her was hidden by the pillar. But she thought the woman's shrug was a work of art.

"Oh, here's my little Heather," Colette drawled. "Say hello to Jarrett, darling. How lovely you looked—and you did such a good job!"

Kit's eyes widened in shock. *Oh, yes,* she thought. *Great job, Heather!* The girl had not only not bothered to warn her about the two models' defection, but she'd nearly ended up on the runway wearing the wrong outfit.

Jarrett Webster's voice was level. "And her fees will cut into the amount you were able to raise for the emergency shelter, I suppose?"

"I'm afraid the results are going to be extremely disappointing," Colette confided. "It's such a worthy cause, too, and it would have been nice for the girls to be able to make a contribution that meant something."

"We worked awfully hard," Heather added. "And I suppose Ms. Deevers did her best, too. But..." Her voice trailed off as if the threesome was moving away.

Kit was livid. The words were true enough, but the

note of doubt in Heather's voice implied that Kit might have sabotaged the show on purpose.

She closed her eyes and concentrated on controlling her breathing and her temper. She told herself it didn't matter what anyone thought as long as she knew she'd done her best. It wasn't her fault that the situation had gone from bad to impossible.

And why should she care what Jarrett Webster believed, anyway? It wasn't as if she wanted to impress him. As far as she was concerned, the man was no more important than a drop of rain in the ocean.

"In fact," she said under her breath, "the very idea of anybody in his line of work raising funds for domestic violence is almost laughable. Unless—I suppose he could have thought the money was to *promote* violence instead of fight it?"

The thought brought a smile, and with a fraction of her self-esteem restored, Kit pushed herself away from the pillar. She was going to change her clothes and go home. Damn Jarrett Webster, anyway. And Heather, and her mother, and all the other debs....

She didn't see him until she crashed directly into his broad chest.

Jarrett caught her by the elbows, preventing her from sprawling on the floor. For a single effortless instant he held her upright, and Kit felt as light and insubstantial as a dandelion seed floating on the wind. Then, efficiently but without gentleness, he set her on her feet.

Bemused, she shot a quick glance at him. Where had he come from? And perhaps more importantly, exactly when? Had he heard what she'd said? Perhaps not. She'd done no more than mutter to herself, and the hall was still noisy. And she certainly hadn't heard *him,* so perhaps...

There was no telling from his expression, she realized.

His brown eyes were chilly, but of course that wasn't any surprise, considering what Heather and Colette had told him. Coming on top of their first encounter, he must think she was an imbecile.

Jarrett Webster's voice was as soft as the silk Kit wore. "I see at least you got that dress on in the right direction."

She lifted her head and stared into his face, determined not to be intimidated. The dress was a beauty, and she knew she didn't look at all bad in it. He had no cause to make nasty cracks.

"Not that it would make a lot of difference," he went on dryly.

Puzzled by his tone, Kit slid a nervous hand over the slender skirt and glanced at the front of the dress.

Her eyes widened in shock. Their collision had knocked her tissue paper stuffing loose. One wad had slid sideways and ended up under her arm, where it resembled a threatening tumor. The other had popped up in the precise center of the low-cut neckline.

"Damn," she said.

For the first time, she saw a glint of humor creep into Jarrett Webster's eyes, but before he had a chance to burst out laughing, Kit turned sharply on her heel and darted toward the dressing room.

Running wasn't her style, but it was just as well she'd acted on the impulse, she told herself as she irritably stripped off the black silk dress. If she'd stayed around another instant, she'd have probably kicked him.

Not that he didn't deserve it.

Kit was running behind schedule on Monday morning. When she arrived for their weekly planning breakfast, her two partners were already sitting in their favorite booth at the restaurant just around the corner from the brownstone that housed Tryad's offices.

Susannah Miller glanced at the dainty watch that dangled on a gold chain around her neck and said, "She's late."

"I noticed." Alison Novak didn't look up from her notebook or stop scribbling. "I wonder if that means she had an exciting weekend."

"No doubt. She thought she was going to meet Jarrett Webster himself, you know. And if she did, and if he's anything like he appears in his ads—"

"You mean maybe she spent the rest of the weekend with him?" Alison considered and shook her head. "No. She'd be even later if that's what happened."

Kit slid into the booth. "I wish you'd stop talking about me as if I'm not here."

"All right," Susannah said agreeably. "So, now that you finally *are* here, tell us what happened. Did you meet the king of lingerie?"

"In the flesh," Kit said. She reached for the lone empty cup, filled it with coffee and savored the aroma. "The trouble is, it was me who was in the flesh—and very little else—at the time."

Susannah blinked. "Darling, you were supposed to be running the fashion show, not modeling for Jarrett Webster. Of course, it might have advantages for the firm. And for you, of course. Does this mean you're going to be his Lingerie Lady next month?"

Kit almost choked on her coffee. "Are you kidding? I hardly fit the profile."

"Well-chosen word," Alison murmured. "They do all seem to have interesting profiles, and we're not talking Roman noses, either." She pulled a glossy fashion magazine from a capacious canvas bag under the table and thrust it at Kit. "I thought you might like to hang this on your office wall."

Kit took the magazine reluctantly. "I didn't know you'd taken to reading this sort of thing."

"Only to keep up with our clients," Alison said repressively.

Susannah looked skyward. "The sacrifices we all make for the sake of business."

"It's just too bad I didn't find it last week or you could have asked him to autograph it."

Kit slid her fingernail down the bright-colored coupon that served as a page marker and opened the magazine. She wasn't surprised at the image that greeted her, even though she'd never seen the photograph before, for all of Milady Lingerie's ads were similar. Each month's campaign featured a new, young and stunningly attractive woman, usually buxom and long-haired—and anonymous. Because the models were never identified by name, everyone called them the Lingerie Ladies.

Each ad included a pair of photographs, spread lavishly over two full pages. The larger, main shot always featured the model provocatively posed and wearing a revealing bit of lingerie. In the other photograph, smaller and usually tucked into a corner of the ad near Milady's distinctive logo, the Lingerie Lady wore street clothes and was pictured with Jarrett Webster—founder, owner and principal designer of Milady Lingerie.

This month's Lingerie Lady was flaxen-haired, with pouting red lips that precisely matched the scarlet satin teddy she was wearing in the main photo. In the smaller shot, she was on the deck of a sailboat leaning against a smiling Jarrett Webster, her windblown hair teasing his tanned face.

"Another blonde," Kit muttered.

"What do you mean?" Susannah craned her neck to see the photo.

"Nothing. It just seems that more often than not lately the Lingerie Ladies are blond."

"I had no idea you were keeping statistics," Susannah murmured.

"I'm not! I just wonder where he finds them all."

"And what he does with all of them after the photo sessions are over? Kitty, darling, you should be ashamed—letting your mind drag in the gutter that way."

Kit would have liked to point out that she hadn't said a thing about Jarrett Webster's conduct, and if anyone's mind needed steam-cleaning it was Susannah's. But if she rose to the bait, Susannah would only smile and declare that the fact Kit hadn't actually said the words didn't mean she hadn't considered the question.

And that was true enough. Practically everyone who'd ever seen a Milady Lingerie ad had spent some time speculating about where Jarrett Webster found those gorgeous women and whether they did more with him than just pose for pictures.

Which, Kit supposed, must have been the main idea of the ad campaign in the first place, for nobody—male or female, redneck or feminist, fan or foe—ever forgot a Milady Lingerie ad.

"Thanks, Ali," she said, and put the coupon carefully in place to mark the page. "I'll post it on my dart board."

Alison's eyebrows rose, but before she could answer the waitress returned with a tray and began setting plates in front of each of them. "We ordered your usual," Alison said, "since we've got a lot of business to cover this morning."

"That's great." Kit buttered her toast and cut into her

garden omelette. "Whose turn is it to keep the meeting on track?"

"Yours," Alison said. "But since both you and Susannah seem to be more interested in Jarrett Webster than in Tryad's new—"

Susannah waved a fork at her. "That's flagrant slander! You're the one who brought the magazine."

"Well, I didn't expect you to count the dots in the picture, either of you." Alison flipped a page in her notebook and said, "Okay, first order of business is to catch up on progress of current projects. How's the art museum fund drive doing, Susannah?"

Susannah stabbed a bite of honeydew melon. "Very well, actually. The Cartwright show opens next month. It's not only the biggest the museum has hung so far, but ticket sales are well beyond what we projected in our original proposal."

Alison frowned. "So you're saying we missed the boat on the estimate?"

"Of course not, Ali. We did a better-than-fantastic job on the promotion, that's all. Don't be fusty."

"All right," Alison said reluctantly. "But keep that factor in mind the next time. While we're writing a proposal is no time to be modest."

"Or overconfident, either," Kit said. "As we were on the fashion show."

"That's next on the list to discuss. How'd it go, Kit? Aside from Jarrett Webster, I mean."

Kit ignored the jab and looked at the bit of toast she held. She hadn't realized she'd shredded it. "It's over," she said. "And believe me, that's the best I can say for the whole event."

She was wrong, of course. It wasn't over. But—fortunately for her—she didn't know that for the better part of three days.

*　*　*

Kit was stretched out on the chaise lounge in the corner of her office, staring at the textured pattern on the ceiling above her head and brainstorming a campaign to publicize a new phone number for a suburban child-abuse hot line, when Susannah put her head around the corner from her own office. "Oh, I'm sorry, I didn't think you were working," she said when she saw Kit's pose, and started to withdraw.

Kit sat up. "I'm not getting anywhere," she admitted. "So come on in. You can pick my brain if I can work on yours."

Susannah grinned. "That's the best bit about having partners, isn't it? What one of us can't think of, the others can. Of course, there's also the fact that we can share celebrations."

Kit looked at her more closely. Susannah's face seemed to glow, and there was a light in her eyes. "Sue, you can't mean Pierce finally got around to proposing?"

"Why couldn't I? Though he didn't, as a matter of fact." She pulled a tall stool away from Kit's drawing board and swiveled it to face the chaise. "It's something wonderful."

"More wonderful than Pierce? I thought—" Too late, Kit saw a shadow drop over Susannah's face, and she would have bit her tongue off if the action would let her take back the careless words. "I'm sorry. What is it, Sue?"

The light reappeared in Susannah's eyes. "He's discovered a fantastic private collection. It's incredible, Kit—a whole group of very valuable paintings, along with some rare pottery and some bits of terrific textiles. And the owner has agreed in principle to donate them to Pierce's museum." She jumped up, obviously unable to sit still. "Just think of all the fun we'll have when it's time to create a publicity campaign to announce *that!*''

''Sounds great—or at least a lot more fun than phone numbers for child-abuse hot lines. Can I help?''

''Of course. I'll need both you and Alison, and every bit of expertise we all have. This is going to be immense, Kit. It's not only a major expansion for the museum, it could mean enormous things for Tryad.'' She struck a ballerina's pose in the center of the office and began to spin.

''Watch it,'' Kit said mildly. ''Keep that up and you'll drill through the floor and end up in the reception room dancing on Rita's desk.''

Susannah laughed, stopped spinning and flopped on the stool once more. ''Who'd have thought five years ago, when you and Alison and I all ended up in that stupid advertising class together, that it would lead to this?''

''Not me,'' Kit said lazily. ''I never even expected to be in public relations, you know.'' It was funny, she thought. Now she couldn't imagine any other way of life. She certainly couldn't contemplate any job that didn't include Susannah and Alison, her own office with its view of the treetops of Lincoln Park and the kind of creative work she loved.

''All the work we've done is starting to pay off in a big way,'' Susannah said with satisfaction.

The intercom on Kit's desk buzzed, and she frowned at it. ''That's funny. I asked Rita not to disturb me for a couple of hours, at least, while I worked out this campaign.''

''My fault,'' Susannah said contritely. ''She must have heard me up here and figured you were finished.''

''Don't fret. Neither of you are interrupting anything important. All I could think of was a bunch of dancing rabbits singing the new phone number, so I suppose that means the real answer will hit me about two in the morning and I'll stay up all night to work out the details." She pushed a button. "Yes, Rita?"

The receptionist's voice was unusually clipped. "There's someone here to see you, Ms. Deevers."

Ms. Deevers? Rita was being awfully formal all of a sudden. Kit's gaze dropped to her calendar, lying open on her desk blotter, and focused on the blank block of time she'd protected specifically for this project. "But I don't have a client scheduled."

"I know," Rita said.

She sounded as if she had something clenched between her teeth, Kit thought. And if Rita, who had twenty years of experience as an executive secretary, reacted that way...

Foreboding dropped over Kit like a mosquito net, whispering down around her, tempting her to try to fight free of its restraint. "I'll be right down."

Kit's office was at the front of the brownstone's second floor, as far as possible from the stairway. She passed Susannah's empty office and paused for an instant at the bottom of the steps to gather her strength and to note the way afternoon light filtered through the stained glass panel above the front door. Then she crossed the narrow hall into what had been the formal parlor when the brownstone was a private home. Now it was Rita's office and the reception room.

Relief flooded the secretary's face as Kit came in, but the concern didn't entirely vanish from her eyes. She looked silently from Kit to a figure in the corner, and Kit followed her gaze.

The man in Rita's office stood with his back to her, apparently studying a framed poster on the wall. He didn't seem to hear her come in.

But Kit didn't need to see his face to know who stood there. In fact, she didn't need to see him at all. The instant she'd stepped through the doorway she'd felt the blast of personal power she'd so quickly come to associate with Jarrett Webster.

She had to clear her throat before she could speak. The necessity annoyed her, and she tried to do it discreetly. But he obviously heard the small noise, and he turned, his movements lazy and graceful, to face her.

Deliberately, Kit did not offer to take him to her office or even to the conference room next door. She stood with one hand on the back of a chair and said coolly, "What can I do for you, Mr. Webster?"

"Oh, it's the other way around entirely."

Kit frowned. "I beg your pardon?"

"I'm here to give *you* something, Ms. Deevers."

Had she left something behind at the fashion show? She wasn't aware of missing anything, except for the poise and decorum she'd sacrificed that afternoon. Or...

Surely he couldn't mean he'd learned how wrong his perceptions had been and had come with an apology!

"Last weekend you had a challenge to face." Jarrett Webster's voice was very deliberate. "And you botched it miserably."

I knew it couldn't be anything as sane and straightforward as an apology, Kit thought. She couldn't help bristling. "I don't think you understand the pressures of working with—"

"I'm not interested in excuses. I'm going to give you a second chance, Ms. Deevers."

"How lovely of you." She didn't bother to keep the sarcasm out of her voice. "Though why you should think I want one—"

"Oh, I don't expect that you do. But it's what you're

getting, nevertheless." He paused and added very gently, "I'm giving you a challenge. You're going to make up for what you wrecked."

CHAPTER TWO

EITHER HER HEARING had gone or the man was a raving lunatic—and there was no doubt in Kit's mind which side of the bet she should put her money on.

She glanced at Rita and found her unabashedly listening. The receptionist was practically leaning over her desk to catch every syllable, and that alone would have told Kit how crazy the situation was. Rita was the perfect secretary, involved and interested but absolutely never nosy. Till now.

"Would you like to come into the conference room, Mr. Webster, so we can discuss this?" Without waiting for an answer, Kit headed for the archway into what had once been the brownstone's dining room. She stopped inside the doors and waited till he'd crossed the threshold.

He paused, eyeing the gleaming finish of the golden oak pocket doors standing half open between the conference room and Rita's office. "Shall I close these for you?"

Kit put a fingertip into the catch of each door and pulled, and the perfectly balanced panels slid into place with no more than a whisper of sound. "Thanks, but I'm perfectly capable." She turned to face him and caught the appraising look in his eyes. Before she could stop herself, she added, "I'm not one of your usual helpless dolls, Mr. Webster."

He didn't rush to answer, and he didn't—as she'd half hoped he might—stop surveying her. "No, you're certainly not."

Kit wished she could believe that was a compliment. Then again, she told herself irritably, if she honestly thought the man was trying to flatter her, she'd be even more furious with him, so she ought to be glad he *hadn't* made that mistake.

"In fact," Jarrett Webster went on, "I'd say you're a woman who's full of surprises. Saturday it was peekaboo blouses and wads of tissue paper, and today—"

Kit didn't want to listen to his opinion of her wardrobe. She'd always liked the simple cut of the cream-colored shirtdress she was wearing—until right this moment, when suddenly it felt as plain as a plastic bag and just as transparent. "I shouldn't think you'd be amazed by that sort of thing."

"Oh, I very seldom see tissue paper put to that use," he assured her.

"I'm quite aware that most of the women you know have chosen figure-enhancing methods more permanent than tissue paper. But as for half-clad females, I'm sure you're an expert."

He considered and nodded. "That's true. And I must say the first thing I noticed about you was that you've got the nicest pair of..."

Kit gasped, tried to smother the sound and choked with the effort. Her eyes started to water, and she could feel herself turning red.

"Shoulder blades I've ever seen," Jarrett finished smoothly. "Why, Ms. Deevers, what *did* you think I was going to say?"

Kit managed, finally, to stop coughing, but the lingering tickle in her throat would have kept her from talking even if she'd had something to say.

"Today, of course, you look amazingly professional."

"Thanks," she managed to say. "I think." She took a firm grip on herself. "If we can get down to business now, Mr. Webster... I do have other projects waiting for my attention.''

"You amaze me." He moved a leather-covered chair out from the conference table and with a graceful turn of his hand invited her to sit.

Kit ignored the gesture and remained on her feet. "It's very kind of you to—what was your offer? Give me a second chance?"

"An opportunity to make good where you failed before," he said helpfully.

"However, Tryad is very busy this season, and I'm afraid we don't have time just now to devote to any more charity fashion shows. You might try us again next year."

Not that it will do you any good, she added to herself. *But at least I'll have twelve months to come up with a good excuse for why I still don't have time.*

Jarrett stood his ground. "You don't seem to understand, Ms. Deevers. This isn't optional."

Kit frowned.

"By the time the fashion show was finished and the costs paid, the grand sum left for fighting domestic abuse was eighty-seven dollars."

Kit shrugged. "Better than nothing, don't you think?"

"A somewhat cynical attitude."

"Perhaps it is—but frankly, I'm astonished there was that much left over."

"Meaning that if you'd expected it, you'd have increased your fee in order to eliminate the excess?"

"Meaning, Mr. Webster, that the entire affair was mismanaged."

"You admit it, then?"

"I'm stating a fact—but it was hardly my fault. Within the constraints of my contract, I did everything I—''

"You were in charge."

"Not entirely, and not from the beginning. By the time I got involved—" But why should she try to explain? It was obvious he wasn't going to take her explanation seriously. He certainly wouldn't take her word over Colette's and Heather's, and Kit would end up sounding as if she was trying to shift the blame onto anyone but herself.

"But you were responsible for the show itself, right?"

Kit hesitated. "That's true."

"A show that was off schedule, out of sync and excruciatingly slow-paced."

"If you're going to compare it to professional affairs, Mr. Webster—"

"I'm not. I know perfectly well it was an amateur event with models who'd never been on a runway before. But it could have been an enjoyable one."

Kit wanted to tell him to talk to the models themselves about that little problem.

"Besides, a large part of the fund-raising effort was focused not on ticket sales but on the reception afterward. The hope was that after an enjoyable show, the guests would donate generously for their refreshments. However, after sitting through that fiasco, two-thirds of them left in disgust rather than stick around to drink tea. Since they weren't present, they didn't contribute, and—"

"I'll take my share of the blame," Kit said honestly.

His eyebrow twitched. "That's refreshing."

"I used very poor judgment. Instead of standing in for the two models who didn't show up, I should have just poked my head out from behind the curtain at the gaps and announced that the ensemble the audience should have been seeing was unavailable because the model was too irresponsible to find a substitute. Would you have liked that any better? I thought not. Look, Mr. Webster, I'm sorry the damned fashion show didn't raise a zillion dollars. But I don't know what you expect me to do about it.''

''That's where the second chance comes in.''

''Now wait a minute! I've told you—''

His voice softened till it felt like warm, rich lotion against her skin. ''Are you afraid you can't meet the challenge, Ms. Deevers?''

''Not in the least. With my hands tied, I could do better than that mishmash of amateur do-gooders did. With a month to work on it, I could raise ten thousand dollars, minimum. But the fact remains that I don't have a month. Tryad can take only a certain amount of time away from our regular client base for nonprofit causes, and we already have all the charity projects we can afford. I'm awfully sorry and all that, but I'm afraid there's nothing I can do. Thanks for stopping by, Mr. Webster.''

Kit could tell from the way his gaze hardened that Jarrett Webster knew a dismissal when he heard it. She was almost surprised, for she doubted he was on the receiving end of a snub very often.

He didn't move, though. Kit walked across the room to the sliding doors, but Jarrett didn't take the hint. He seemed to be as firmly planted in the conference room as a willow tree on the bank of a pond, and his words dropped into the silence with the same effect as a rock into water. ''I'll pay for your time.''

With one hand on the pocket door, Kit turned in astonishment. ''What?''

''I said, I'll foot the bills—not only the charges for your time, at your regular rates, but the basic costs of whatever event you create.''

''Why?''

He didn't answer. ''Your challenge is to raise enough

money above and beyond those costs to show me that you're not incompetent, after all.''

"Why not just give your money directly to a shelter somewhere?"

"Are you saying you can't do it?"

"Of course not. But I don't understand why—"

"Because you're going to take my money and multiply it. Instead of giving, say, a couple of thousand dollars directly, I invest it with you, and you'll turn it into— What was it you said? Ten thousand, minimum? In a month?"

"I may have said that, but—"

"Backing down, Ms. Deevers?" He shook his head sadly. "I'm disappointed in you. It's such a worthy cause, you see. And besides, if you don't take this challenge—"

Kit wanted to ignore him, but the question hung in the air like a plume of toxic gas, threatening to choke and smother her. "What if I don't?"

"If you don't succeed, or if you don't even have the guts to try, then I will take great pleasure in telling everyone I deal with exactly why Tryad is a good firm to stay away from."

Kit gasped. "That's not fair!"

"If you don't believe in your abilities, Ms. Deevers, why should I cut you any slack? I think I'd be doing a public service, frankly, to let your prospective clients know what they're getting into."

"That's not what I mean. It's not fair to blame Tryad as a whole for something that was my doing."

"I thought," he said gently, "that you said it wasn't your fault."

"It wasn't, but at least I was involved. My partners weren't. It has absolutely nothing to do with them."

Jarrett shrugged. "You're part of this firm, so whatever you do reflects on them."

"Yes, but—" She stumbled to a halt, unable to think of a telling argument.

"Take it or leave it." Finally, he moved, striding with the easy grace of a lynx toward the door where she stood. "I'll leave my card with your receptionist." The sleeve of his linen blazer brushed Kit's bare arm. The contact stung as if she'd been whipped with nettles.

"Wait!"

He turned. He was less than a foot from her, and Kit had to look a long way up into his face. There were flecks of gold in his dark brown eyes, and tiny lines at the corners. Those must come from the time he spent on that sailboat with the current Lingerie Lady.

"Your complaint is with me," she said desperately. "Not with Tryad. So I'll make you a deal."

He shrugged. "You're not exactly in a good place to be dictating terms, you know."

"I'll do a campaign for you, and I'll do my best to raise at least ten thousand dollars."

"Somehow," Jarrett mused, "this sounds familiar. Almost as if I'd said it myself."

"But I'll do it on my own time. You don't have to pay me a dime, but in return, you have to promise that Tryad doesn't come into it."

He looked thoughtful. "You mean, you want me to promise that if you fail—"

"I won't fail!"

"In that case," he said gently, "you—and Tryad—don't have a thing to worry about, do you? Shall we shake hands on our deal, Ms. Deevers?"

Kit didn't walk him to the front door, as all three of the partners usually did with their clients. Mostly, she admitted, it was because she wasn't so sure she could still walk.

She heard the front door close and sank against the conference room wall with a thud. How had he managed to turn things so neatly against her? She'd made a perfectly reasonable proposition, and he'd shot it down without even bothering to take aim.

She wanted to pound her forehead against the door.

A couple of minutes later Susannah came in. "He's gorgeous," she said.

"I suppose you were hovering in the hallway so you could get a good look?"

"Of course not," Susannah said with dignity. "I was supervising Rita's typing."

"Bet she loved having you leaning over her shoulder."

"I wasn't. I was sitting on her desk—I had a much better view of the conference room door that way. Kit, he's twice as terrific as his pictures. No wonder you... Are you all right?"

"Just jolly," Kit said under her breath.

"Well, good. You look a little stunned, though. Let me guess what happened. He was so impressed by you that he wants Tryad to take over Milady Lingerie's public relations?"

"It has nothing to do with Tryad." *And it's up to me to keep it that way,* Kit reminded herself. *I have a month to raise ten thousand dollars or...*

No, she reminded herself. She *didn't* have a month. She had only her personal time—whatever remained after her normal workload. The only thing she'd succeeded in doing with the brash bargain she'd tried to make was to cheat herself. If she'd kept her mouth shut, at least he'd have been paying for her time, and she'd have a full thirty days to pull this off.

But at least, she thought, the fact that she wasn't getting a cent out of the deal meant that she'd have less money to raise overall. Perhaps, if she tried hard enough, she could convince herself that was a positive note.

"You mean..." Susannah gave a shriek that rattled the brass and crystal chandelier above the conference table. "Then he was asking you for a *date?*"

Alison's head appeared around the door. "I can hear you two all the way in my office," she pointed out. "What in heaven's name is going on in here? And if it's some sort of party, why didn't you invite me to join in the fun?"

"Because it just happened," Susannah said. "Very unexpectedly. Jarrett Webster popped in out of the blue and—"

"Did *not* ask me for a date," Kit cut in hastily. "Look, this is private and personal, and I really don't want to—"

Susannah nodded wisely at Alison. "She doesn't want to talk about it."

"Do you think that means she has something to hide?"

"No doubt. I'll have to think what the secret might be, though. If it isn't business and it isn't a date, then—"

"Stop it!" Kit said firmly. "Both of you!" She turned sideways to slide between them and out the door, and the last view she had as she started up the stairs was of two astonished faces in the doorway of Rita's office.

Then the irrepressible Susannah said, "Kit's just a little touchy today, wouldn't you say, Ali? I wonder if that means she's in love?"

Forty-eight slow and painful hours crept by. By Friday afternoon, Kit still hadn't heard from Jarrett, and she was beginning to hope that somewhere, somehow, someone had told him what had really happened to mess up the fashion show. If he learned that she hadn't been responsible for the mix-ups...

Not likely, she told herself. Who was going to admit it, after all? Not Heather, that was sure, or her mother. And neither chance nor divine providence was apt to step in to change his mind and rescue her, either.

Even if he did learn the truth, Kit might not be entirely off the hook. Unless he was man enough to apologize, which she frankly doubted, she might not even find out that he'd seen the light.

And in the meantime, she didn't dare take a chance on waiting. She couldn't put off the necessary work for another moment.

She'd opened her big mouth and now she was going to have to back up her boast with action. Three lousy weeks and ten thousand dollars to raise.

Kit knew all the tricks. Professional fund-raising wasn't particularly difficult, and in a city the size of Chicago ten thousand dollars wasn't a great deal of money, either. Except that it was a whole lot more difficult to raise money for an amorphous general cause like fighting domestic violence than for a specific one like putting a new roof on a women's shelter. Why couldn't the man have been more precise?

"Because," Kit muttered, "it would have been helpful if he had, and he knows it."

So how was she going to pull it off?

Susannah, she knew, could come up with that amount in a matter of days for her favorite museum—but the museum had a mailing list of supporters. And a couple of months ago Alison had reached out and touched Chicago's corporate trusts and charitable foundations, and in mere hours she'd raised enough money to fund a video production on the benefits of living and working in the Windy City.

Kit had her contacts, too, but she didn't think simply calling them up to ask for money would be likely to solve this problem. She suspected Jarrett wouldn't be particularly thrilled if she handed him a few big checks. Too easy, he'd probably say. The money would no doubt have been donated anyway, without her interference.

That would be a technical success for Kit, but one that wouldn't mean much. Under those circumstances, Jarrett might not actually carry through with his threat to use his contacts against Tryad. But unless he was wholeheartedly convinced, he certainly wouldn't do the firm any favors, either. And if a man with Jarrett Webster's influence and power so much as raised an eyebrow when Tryad was mentioned...

"Let's face it," Kit muttered. "He doesn't have to bad-mouth us. All he has to do is sow a little doubt. A cynical question here and a hesitant look there, and our clients will start looking for cover."

The fact was, Kit realized, that raising the money she'd promised wasn't really the primary goal of this campaign. Impressing Jarrett Webster was, because if she didn't succeed in swaying him, she'd lose the battle—no matter how much money she handed over to his precious cause.

The good news, she told herself, *is that you don't have to impress him on any personal level.* Considering the way she'd started out, that would be downright impossible.

She reached for a pencil and a pad of graph paper and wrote in block letters across the top, How to excite Jarrett Webster.

Then she stared at the blank page and tapped the eraser against her cheek.

New money—that was what she needed to set the arrogant Mr. Webster on his heels. If she could come up with ten thousand dollars from ordinary people who otherwise wouldn't have made a donation, money that would have been spent on *things* instead of good causes...

Her pencil moved slowly across the page, doodling a row of parallel lines.

She needed an event that would grab publicity—a month wasn't long enough for a slow-building campaign. It had to be something flashy to intrigue the fickle public. And it must return entertainment or actual value to the contributors so they wouldn't mind handing over fairly large sums of hard-earned money.

All of which was precisely what the fashion show had tried to do, she reminded herself. Well, she wasn't stupid enough to try that again. But there were plenty of activities people would pay to attend. A formal ball, perhaps—though there must be a dozen already planned for the next few months. A banquet. A rock concert or maybe a symphony performance.

She could feel her blood pressure inching up. There was nothing particularly intriguing about any of those possibilities, certainly nothing that would generate the sort of publicity she needed.

Her intercom buzzed, and Rita announced, "Telephone, Kit. Line three."

With a tinge of relief Kit tossed the graph paper aside. But as soon as she picked up the receiver, she knew who was waiting for her. Her fingertips began to tingle, and by the time she'd said hello the sensation had rushed all the way up her arm and leaped to her throat. Did the man give off an electrical current that had the power to surge through telephone lines and paralyze whoever was on the other end?

Jarrett didn't bother to return her greeting. "When do you get off work?"

I don't, Kit wanted to say. *I'm going to stay here in my office forever, working round the clock like a galley slave for the rest of my life.* "I'll be finished in half an hour."

"I'll be waiting in front."

The telephone clicked in her ear before she could argue. Or agree, for that matter.

Calling that man arrogant, she fumed, was an understatement of approximately the same magnitude as referring to the Great Chicago Fire as a backyard wiener roast!

One thing was certain. There hadn't been anything in his voice that hinted of regret or apology. So was there any reason she should stick around? Since he hadn't even let her answer his demand, much less tell him whether it was convenient to meet with him right now...

No, she decided. She shoved the pad of graph paper into her briefcase, along with a dozen folders containing other current projects, took her trench coat from its hook, wrapped a bright wool scarf around her throat and tried not to look as if she was hurrying as she descended the stairs to the front door. With any luck, she could be around the corner and out of sight before he arrived—and all the way home before the half hour was up.

Though she should give him a smidgen of credit, Kit decided. At least he'd had the decency to offer to wait outside. He could have come in and started Susannah speculating again.

Kit glanced up as she reached the front walk, and her steps slowed. Parked by the fireplug directly in front of the brownstone was a shiny black Porsche, and leaning against the passenger door, arms folded patiently, stood Jarrett Webster.

"You said half an hour," he pointed out.

Kit felt herself coloring guiltily.

"It's a good thing I called from my car, isn't it?" he went on. "Sneaking out like that, Ms. Deevers. One would think you didn't want to talk to me."

"If you'd stayed on the phone a moment longer, I would have told you that I have other plans for the evening."

"Then I'm glad I didn't. This shouldn't take all evening, anyway. Or did you think I was asking for a date?"

"Heaven forbid," Kit said under her breath.

"Good. I'm glad we've got that straight. I'm here for a progress report."

"What makes you think I want to give you one?"

"See? I told you our conversation wouldn't take long. Does that mean you haven't anything to tell me?"

"No, it means I don't want to tell you about my plans till I have the details worked out," Kit said. That was perfectly true, she told herself, even though it wasn't quite factual—implying as it did that she had everything but the details in mind.

She added honestly, "Since I hadn't heard from you in a couple of days, I thought perhaps you had second thoughts about the whole project."

"I do have a business to run and a deadline for the designs for next year's collections. And I don't expect even you—public relations genius that you seem to be—"

The irony in his voice was so thick Kit thought she could have sliced it.

"To come up with a plan without a chance to think it through. But you should know that I'm not known for changing my mind once I've made it up."

"There are those who'd say that's not determination but pure rigidity," Kit said sweetly.

He smiled. "I suppose that depends on which side you find yourself on. At any rate, I thought I should find out what you were planning before you got too deeply into your preparations."

"In case you don't want your name associated with my idea? Now there's a thought." From the corner of her eye Kit saw the flutter of a lace curtain in the bay window of the brownstone next door, the twin to Tryad's office. Automatically, she lifted a hand to wave.

"Friend of yours?" he asked.

"Not exactly. None of us have ever actually met her. She just watches us all the time." Mrs. Holcomb's close observation reminded her that Susannah and Alison would probably be leaving soon. The last thing she needed was for them to catch her schmoozing with Jarrett on the front sidewalk.

"It wasn't that I expected you to try to embarrass me," he went on. "I just didn't want you to waste a whole weekend of your precious month working on a scheme that I might not approve."

"Weekend?" Kit was disgusted with herself. How had she managed to forget it was Friday night? Not only would Susannah and Alison be leaving work soon, but they'd be expecting her to meet them at the neighborhood bar where they stopped every Friday night for bratwurst and a chance to discuss the week.

"Look," she said briskly, "I told you I have plans. Maybe we could meet tomorrow?"

He shook his head. "I'll be tied up."

Kit told herself not to take the comment literally, but she couldn't help it. Would next month's Lingerie Lady be pictured in black leather, standing over a bound and handcuffed Jarrett Webster? The idea had its attractions. "Of course your plans are more important than mine," she murmured. "All right, I suppose I could spare a few minutes. Would you like a cup of coffee? There's a little restaurant around the corner.''

His eyes narrowed. "You're suddenly very eager to chat." But he dropped into step beside her without arguing.

They had to pass Flanagan's, where the scent of bratwurst was wafting through the propped-open front door and out to the street. A textbook example of good public relations, Alison always called it—the subtlest form of advertising.

Kit thought Jarrett sniffed appreciatively, and she held her breath till they were well past, half-expecting that he'd suggest they stop for bratwurst and beer instead.

Inside the coffee shop, Kit led the way to a booth at the back and took the seat facing the door. "Two coffees," she told the waitress. "Unless you'd like something else?"

"It's your party," he said.

The coffee arrived and Kit stirred cream into her cup. "I'm puzzled," she said finally. "Why are you doing this? I can't imagine why you have such a hate for Tryad—"

"I don't, particularly. But fair's fair."

"Exactly. That's why I didn't charge the fashion show people a fee, just expenses."

He shrugged. "I can't see that it matters much. The result was the same, whatever you called it."

So much for the attempt to reason with him, Kit thought.

"So tell me what you're going to do," he suggested. "I won't hold you to the details just yet, but I need to know when this affair is coming off so I can fit it into my calendar."

"I'd hate to put you to the trouble. Besides, who says I need a special date? Perhaps I'll just send out a chain letter.'' Where the notion had come from, Kit didn't know, but almost instantly she warmed to the idea. ''You know the kind—'Send a hundred dollars to the name at the top of the list, and within seven days make six copies of this letter and send them out to your friends. Before the month is out, you'll receive—'''

His voice was dry. ''Oh, that sounds as if it has real potential.''

Kit pretended to take him seriously. ''Doesn't it, though? I wonder how long it would take. If I make all the names on the original list dummies, so the money from the first few levels comes back to me...''

''Why would people send money for a scam like that?''

''Have you no imagination?'' Kit smiled warmly at him. ''I'll threaten to send someone from the domestic abuse foundation to beat them up if they don't. Let's see, if the first twelve all send out letters...'' She reached for a paper napkin from the holder on the table and started to scribble. Two calculations later she was hopelessly lost.

''They won't. Even with threats you'd be lucky to get half.''

''Really?'' Kit looked at the muddle of figures on the napkin and pushed it aside. ''I'll still bet in a month I'd have ten thousand dollars.''

He looked thoughtful. ''Assuming a fifty percent response, in three generations—which is all you'd have time for—you'd take in just short of eight thousand.''

''You did that all in your head, didn't you?'' Kit said admiringly. ''Well, I'll take your word for it. Eight thousand dollars—and at the cost of only a dozen stamps. Not a bad return on an investment. If we let it go one more round—''

"You're putting a lot of faith in the postal service, of course—assuming that all that mail gets delivered."

"There is that difficulty."

"And, of course, there's the minor problem that it's illegal to send chain letters through the mail."

"I was afraid you'd remember that," Kit admitted. "It was still a good idea, though." She crumpled the napkin.

"So, since the chain letter was obviously a sham, what are you really going to do?"

"Are you this big a spoilsport with your ad agency? I must say I have trouble picturing you meekly doing everything they suggest for those ads of yours. The one where you were pretending to be on safari, for instance—"

"That was a real tiger, even if the only shooting was done with cameras. A fan of my ads, are you?"

Oops, Kit told herself. *That was a slip.* "Not at all. It's just that they're a bit difficult to avoid. One would have to quit reading altogether to escape them, and even then there are the billboards."

He drained his cup and set it on the table with a firm click. "Let's get down to it, Ms. Deevers. Obviously you don't have an idea in your head about this fund-raiser. So why don't you just admit it?"

"Why should I?" she asked cautiously.

"Because we may as well call the whole thing off now, before you make a fool of yourself."

Kit felt a slow burn start in her toes and work up. "You sound awfully sure I'm the one who'll look foolish."

"I didn't say that."

"No—now that I think about it, you didn't. I wonder if that means you're afraid I'll succeed and you'll have to eat crow."

"That possibility doesn't seem likely."

"I'll call it off if you'll promise to keep your mouth shut about Tryad."

"You're not dictating the terms here, Ms. Deevers."

"Really? Well, no dice." She eased out of the booth. "I won't give you the satisfaction of telling people I backed out, and you're not going to slander my company, either. I'm going to pull this off, Mr. Damn-Your-Arrogance Webster—and you're going to be so impressed by the time it's over that you not only won't run down Tryad, you'll give us referrals."

He didn't move. "Pull it off and you have my promise—all the referrals I can manage. Of course, in the meantime, I can't wait to hear all about how you're going to do it."

Neither can I, Kit thought. *So now, all I have to do is figure it out.*

CHAPTER THREE

ALISON was already in Flanagan's when Kit arrived. She was sitting at a table toward the back of the dim little pub, taking advantage of the light from a neon beer sign above her head to read the latest issue of a public relations journal.

The glass of diet cola in Alison's hand was half empty, Kit saw. That meant she'd been there for a while, and since she wasn't in a position to look out the front window there was no chance she'd seen Kit walking by with Jarrett.

One down, Kit thought.

Kit pulled out a chair across from her partner and waved at the waitress. "Where's Susannah?"

"Don't know." Alison slid a bar napkin into the magazine to mark her page and set it aside. "She had a meeting with a client this afternoon, and she wasn't back yet when I left."

"If it was Pierce at the museum, she might not be back at all." The waitress brought Kit a glass of Chardonnay, and she sipped it gratefully.

Alison looked puzzled. "You don't think she's serious about him, do you?"

"Why shouldn't she be? I've only met him a couple of times, but he seems nice enough, and he's certainly attractive."

"He's not her type. Look at me in disbelief if you want, Kit, but underneath all that froth, our Susannah's a very steady sort. And somehow, I suspect, Pierce isn't.

42

She's no more serious about him than...than you are about Jarrett Webster.''

Kit almost choked. "Oh, well, when you put it that way..." She drew a set of imaginary parallel lines on the tabletop with the base of her wineglass. "Ali, if you had to raise a lot of money for a good cause in a very little time, what would you do?''

"Is this a trick question, or wasn't I listening at our staff meeting Monday?''

"It came up since then. It's sort of a competition.'' At least that much was the truth, Kit thought.

Alison looked thoughtful, but before she could comment Susannah came in with a swirl of her jersey skirt and sank into the chair across from Kit. "Guess what I just saw, parked straight in front of the brownstone. The most gorgeous black Porsche with Teddy on the license plates. Putting two and two together—''

"And coming up with seven, no doubt,'' Alison said. "I thought incredible math was Kit's specialty.''

"Maybe the car belongs to a bear collector,'' Kit said.

Susannah leaned forward. "Then what was Jarrett Webster doing walking down the street toward it?''

"Taking a healthy stroll?'' Kit mused. "Or slumming, perhaps?''

"You really don't know?'' Susannah sounded doubtful. "I thought perhaps he was looking for you, but Rita said he hadn't come into the office.''

"See, Kit? I told you Susannah wasn't serious about Pierce. In fact, it's beginning to sound as if she's got Jarrett Webster on the brain, instead.''

Susannah rolled her eyes. "Ali, you know very well I wouldn't poach on Kit's territory.''

"You're welcome to him,'' Kit offered.

"You two and your men,'' Alison grumbled.

Susannah sat up straight. "Oh? As if there aren't any in your life?"

"The men in my life are friends, not romantic interests. And now that we're on the subject—"

"I'm lost," Susannah said. "Which subject? Friends or romantic interests?"

"Friends. Two of mine are announcing their engagement tomorrow evening. The party came up rather suddenly, and—"

"And you want to know what to take as a gift? I'd suggest a bottle of champagne. That's always appreciated." Susannah flagged the waitress. "I don't know about you two, but I'm starving."

"Thanks, darling, but I can figure out a gift," Alison said. "The trouble is, I'm also supposed to attend a convention banquet for one of our clients. It's not critically important, I suppose—I mean, I'll stop by the convention during the day, and it's not as if we're in charge of the arrangements for the banquet itself. But I think Tryad ought to be represented, so I was wondering if one of you—"

Susannah shook her head. "Sorry, but I've already made plans for the whole weekend."

"I'll go," Kit said. "Tell me where and when."

"You're a love, Kitty. I owe you one." Alison passed an envelope across the table. "Here are the tickets. It's at the Englin Hotel, main ballroom, eight o'clock."

"Tickets?" Susannah said. "Plural?"

"Too late, Kit's got dibs. And you've already got plans, remember?"

"I didn't mean I was volunteering to take over. I just couldn't help thinking of who Kit might take. As long as there's an extra ticket—"

"I can't think of a soul I want to spend the evening with," Kit said firmly. "At least, not one I could invite to a banquet featuring rubbery chicken and a roomful of strangers.''

"That's a curse of modern life, you know," Susannah announced. "Somebody ought to start up a singles club."

"I hate to burst your bubble, dear," Alison said, "but someone already has."

"No, I mean a real singles club—not a dating service, but something to deal with the honest-to-goodness problems of unattached life. The woman who needs a companion for a dull evening at a business banquet, the man who doesn't know how to do his own laundry—"

"I think you've just hit on the reason it won't work." Kit tucked the envelope into an inside pocket of her handbag.

"I didn't say she should actually wash his shirts, just teach him how."

"I told you Susannah's a very conservative type, underneath it all," Alison murmured. "Next thing we know, she'll be starting up a Laundromat."

Kit tried not to laugh at the indignant look on Susannah's face. *I do love these two,* she thought. *And I can't let them, or Tryad, down.*

Kit spent a restless night, and as dawn approached, dreams disturbed her. Aware enough to know she wasn't awake but unable to pull herself from the nightmare, she lay rigid as one weird scene chased another through her mind. Finally, just as Jarrett Webster triumphantly put Tryad out of business and began to personally auction off everything from desks to copy machines to drawing boards to the calico cat who lived in the top-floor production room, Kit woke with a snap.

She lay flat on her back, her heart pounding painfully. A couple of tears had slipped from the corners of her eyes and lost themselves in the soft brown hair at her temples. But she felt more anger than fear.

She pushed herself upright and went to the kitchenette. While she waited for her coffee to brew, she relived the dream, analyzing each unrealistic element in the hope of banishing the emotional hangover it had left behind. She still felt half dazed.

It was only a nightmare, after all, she told herself, the aftereffects of contact with an arrogant, insufferable, egotistical male.

"I'd like to auction *him!*" she said, and the coffeemaker sighed as if in agreement.

She started to fill her cup and stopped, holding the pot in midair. *And why not?* she asked herself.

She stood frozen in place, not seeing the stream of coffee that overflowed her cup and pooled on the kitchen counter.

There were women who'd love to spend an evening with Jarrett Webster. Kit recognized the attraction he posed, even though she didn't understand it. He wasn't to her taste, but there was no question he was devastatingly good-looking, and that aura of power was no doubt a turn-on for a lot of women. Add his money and his fame....

Yes, there were women masochistic enough to pay for the privilege of spending an evening with him. Why shouldn't Kit—and a good cause, of course—take advantage of the phenomenon?

"Bachelor auction," she said dreamily. "A date with Jarrett Webster, sold to the highest bidder."

It wouldn't work, of course. He'd have to cooperate to make the idea fly, and Jarrett's ego was far too large to allow him to take a chance on having to spend an evening with a woman who didn't meet his standards. But if he refused...

He could still hurt Tryad, she reflected. Unless Kit could manipulate him into making that refusal so publicly, so blatantly, so unreasonably that it would ruin his credibility where she and Tryad were concerned.

Kit mopped up the spill and drank her coffee without tasting it while she plotted the most effective way to embarrass Jarrett Webster in public.

The Englin Hotel was one of the city's oldest and grandest, and Kit had always thought the baroque main ballroom one of the most beautiful in existence. It bore no resemblance to the sterile meeting rooms of more modern hotels. With its cream and gold walls and the hand-painted clouds and cupids on the lofty arched ceiling, this was a room full of elegance.

It was wasted on the typical dull awards banquet, Kit thought. The room should be reserved for grand balls. It seemed to cry out for hoopskirts and masks, feathers and fans, not the staid dark business suits most of tonight's crowd were wearing.

Still, she'd enjoy the surroundings, even if she wasn't likely to be absorbed in the business of the evening. As long as she looked politely interested, she could devote her attention to putting the finishing touches on her plan for Jarrett.

When she presented her ticket at the door, the ballroom was bustling with manufacturers of all ages and types. Three massive gold and crystal chandeliers cast a soft glow over the white-draped tables, each set for ten diners. Waiters were setting out fruit cups as the guests coming into the ballroom sought out their places.

"You'll be at table twelve," the hostess at the ballroom door told Kit as she checked Alison's name off her list. "Seats five and six."

"I don't have a guest," Kit said. "So if you need the extra chair—"

But the hostess had already turned to greet the next couple. Kit tucked the ticket envelope into her tiny handbag and walked into the ballroom. A shiver ran up her spine, reminiscent of the first time she'd seen this room as an awestruck teenager attending her first truly formal dance. Tonight, however, the reason for her reaction was more mundane. The ballroom was downright cold. The temperature would soon moderate, Kit knew, with a couple of thousand warm bodies filling the place. But in the meantime, she was glad she'd brought along a shawl.

She paused inside the door to drape the soft, cream-colored Irish wool around her shoulders and happened to spot a familiar face nearby. One of the Englin's concierges was giving instructions to a platoon of waiters. As he finished, he caught Kit's eye and smiled, and as soon as the waiters rushed off to follow orders, he came toward the door to greet her.

She finished settling her shawl and held out a hand. "Hello, Carl. I haven't seen you in ages. I thought you'd moved on to bigger things than nursemaiding banquets."

He rolled his eyes. "I thought so, too. I inherited this one at the last minute. Though perhaps I should be careful what I say, in case you're the one who planned the thing."

Kit smiled. "No, thank heaven. Alison's done some public relations work for the company, but they hired a specialist to arrange the entire convention. I'm just here to represent her at the party."

"Lucky you." His gaze slid away from her to roam the ballroom.

There was a tinge of irony in his voice, but Kit thought she was lucky, indeed. She'd expected to have to wait till Monday morning to put the first stage of her plan into effect, but this chance meeting was like a plum dropped into her lap. "Carl, you wouldn't happen to know if the hotel has a room available three weeks from tonight, would you?"

"The ballroom, you mean? I doubt it. It's a rare Saturday night we don't have a convention or a wedding reception. I can look at the reservations book, but I think—"

"Oh, no," Kit said hastily. "I need space for a hundred people, perhaps—not two thousand."

"That won't be quite as difficult. Can you call me Monday morning to check for sure? I'll be here." His eyes narrowed as he focused on a far corner of the ballroom, and Kit wondered what potential trouble he'd spotted. "In fact," he added dryly, "at the rate things are going tonight, I might *still* be here."

"Monday," Kit confirmed. Carl moved away, and she glanced around the ballroom, looking for table twelve.

A low, rich voice spoke behind her. "What's happening on Monday?"

Kit jumped, and her shawl slid off one shoulder as she spun to face the last person she'd expected to confront tonight, almost forty-eight hours before she was ready for him. "Do you specialize in sneaking up on people?" she snapped.

A thoughtful gleam sprang to life in Jarrett's dark eyes.

Kit could have bitten off her tongue. Would she never learn to stop and think before speaking?

He shrugged, and she could almost see the easy flow of muscles under the perfectly tailored black tuxedo. A different one than he'd been wearing at the fashion show, Kit knew, though men's evening clothes were all so similar that she didn't quite understand why she was so certain. She didn't care for the idea that she'd been paying such close attention to details like the width of his lapels.

Though perhaps that was better than paying close attention to *him*, she told herself.

"All I did was walk in," he said gently. He stretched out a hand to capture the errant corner of her shawl and draped the soft wool around her shoulders once more. "You're the one who was chatting in the middle of the main aisle where anyone might overhear. So if you're feeling spied upon, I suppose the real question is what are you up to that's caused you to feel—"

"I'm not paranoid, Mr. Webster."

"I was going to say *guilty*, but if you'd prefer your definition, I suppose—"

She decided not to argue the point. "What are you doing here, anyway? I wouldn't have thought this was your kind of thing."

"Banquets and conventions? One learns to put up with a certain number of them. Of course, I had no idea this one would turn out to be a thriller." His gaze wandered lazily down the length of her, taking in everything from sparkly crystal earrings to high-heeled pumps.

At least, Kit thought, *I don't need to worry about misplaced tissue paper tonight!*

"So what are you planning for Monday?" he went on. "You seem to have overlooked answering my question."

"Noticed that, did you? You're being very acute tonight. What *does* bring you here? These people manufacture bridge girders and steel cables. It's hardly in your line of work."

"Oh, I don't know," he said easily. "I suppose you could say we're all in the business of support."

On the podium, the emcee tested the microphone, and a moment later the lights dimmed.

Jarrett slid a hand under Kit's elbow. "Shall we find your table before we get lost in the dark?"

At least, Kit told herself, she wasn't cold anymore. Just the idea of being lost in the dark with him was enough to pump steam through her veins. No doubt about it, the sooner she got safely to her place—and Jarrett went away—the better off she'd be. So she allowed him to draw her closer to his side to squeeze between the closely packed tables.

"I'm at number twelve," she said. "But I can find it on my own, thanks."

He shook his head. "Oh, no. I heard you say you had an extra ticket and no one to use it."

He'd been standing behind her as she talked to the hostess, close enough to overhear? But she hadn't felt his presence, Kit thought. Then she realized how silly that sounded—as if he transmitted radio waves and she was specially tuned to receive them!

"It would be a shame to have an empty seat next to you," Jarrett went on smoothly, "so I'll happily fill in."

Kit gritted her teeth and managed to say, "How thoughtful of you to consider my comfort."

The corner of his mouth twitched upward. "Oh, think nothing of it," he said earnestly. "The whole event is being videotaped, and so close to the podium, an empty chair would really stand out. We can't have that."

Kit wanted to stick her tongue out at him, but she caught his sidelong glance at her and knew he was hoping for something of the sort. She settled for pretending that he hadn't spoken at all. "It's very kind of you to make the sacrifice of sitting next to me. But I'm sure you already have a seat somewhere else."

"Actually, I don't."

Kit feigned a frown. "Does that mean you're crashing the party? I had no idea you led such a dull life that

you'd seek out events like this. One would think that in
your position you could find all sorts of entertainment—''

"I'm on the board of directors of the group that's
hosting this party."

"Of course," Kit murmured.

"And the directors are floating tonight, filling in
wherever we're needed and making sure everyone feels
welcome and comfortable." He intercepted a passing
waiter, lifted two glasses of champagne from the man's
tray and handed one to Kit. *"Salud."*

"Well, if you really want to make sure I have a good
time—'' Kit sipped her champagne and smiled sweetly
at him ''—go away.''

Jarrett laughed. "But I can't. There's still the problem
of the empty chair. Oh, here's table twelve." He seated
Kit with a flourish and pulled out the chair next to hers,
the last remaining unoccupied one at the table.

The barrel-chested man sitting next to Kit leaned
across her to extend a massive hand toward Jarrett.
"Anderson's the name. Good to see you again,
Webster—we met in New Orleans a year or so ago.
Who's this with you?" Kit almost choked on the wave
of Scotch on the man's breath before he released Jarrett's
hand and leaned back in his chair, grinning at her. "I
get it. We're going to get a preview of the newest
Lingerie Lady, right?"

That sort of idiocy wasn't any big surprise, Kit
thought. With the load of Scotch he must have already
consumed, the man was probably seeing double, so it
was no wonder he wasn't thinking clearly, either. The
very idea that she might be the next half-clad beauty in
Jarrett's ads was insane.

"Hardly," Jarrett said coolly.

Annoyance rose in Kit's throat till it threatened to

choke her. *You're being completely irrational,* she told herself. She certainly didn't think of herself as the sort of bimbo who'd be interested in appearing in one of those slinky, sexist ads even if she had the body for it—which nobody had ever suggested she had. So why should she be furious when Jarrett made it clear he didn't think of her in those terms, either? She ought to be flattered.

But whether it was reasonable or not, she still wanted to slug him.

"Not that she couldn't be," Jarrett added calmly. "Under the right circumstances."

Kit gritted her teeth. She could just about hear what was coming next—a list of all the steps necessary to turn plain and simple Kit Deevers into Lingerie Lady material. An implant here, a tuck there, a haircut and a bleach job...

Kit's hand clenched on the stem of her champagne flute. *I swear,* she thought, if he starts, *I'll dump this glass on his head—and I hope the videotape is running.*

Jarrett's fingertip stroked the tendons that stood out white on the back of her hand. "But right now I prefer to keep her to myself."

The soft, almost intimate tone of his voice, the gentle touch of his fingertip against her skin, seemed to rob Kit of the power of motion. Since when, she wondered, had the perfectly utilitarian tendons in the back of her hand turned into an erotic zone?

"Oh, is that the secret of how you choose your models, Mr. Webster?" asked the woman sitting next to Jarrett. "The ad is the way you say goodbye to women when they go out of your life?"

Kit cleared her throat. "And that's why you shouldn't expect to see me in the magazines anytime soon, because—"

Jarrett's eyes widened theatrically. "Because you don't intend to go out of my life? My dear—"

"Because you have yet to get past hello," Kit said firmly. "To say nothing of the fact that I wouldn't be caught dead in one of those outfits you specialize in."

"Careful, Ms. Deevers. I might conclude you're issuing a challenge."

The laughter in his voice felt like salt against a fresh wound. "I wouldn't waste my time doing anything so foolish." Kit's voice was sweet. "You couldn't possibly be any less interested in me—no matter what I was wearing—than I am in you."

"No doubt," he said thoughtfully, "you're right."

The laughter was gone from his voice, and the fact left Kit feeling almost deflated. When he turned to the woman on his right—the woman who'd made the catty comment about his models—and asked a polite question about what company connection had brought her to the banquet, Kit swallowed hard and tried to concentrate on her fruit cup.

What did you expect? she asked herself. *And what did you want, anyway? Certainly not any more of that kind of silliness!*

The drunk at her left elbow kept leaning closer. By the main course he was practically in Kit's lap. With her appetite gone, she laid her steak knife across her plate—a better idea in the long run than burying it in the drunk's ribs, she told herself—and shifted as far away from him as possible.

Unfortunately, that put her almost against Jarrett's side. Very casually, without even looking at her, he draped an arm around her shoulders. His fingertips slipped through the loose knit of her shawl and teased the soft skin of her bare arm.

To an onlooker, Kit thought irritably, the gesture must

look like that of a satisfied lover, one who knew his touch would be welcomed. The casually possessive arm wasn't all that annoyed her, however. She thought Jarrett might as well have announced that he didn't believe she could stand up for herself.

The drunk, however, took one look at that possessive arm and backed off, leaving Kit torn between relief and aggravation. She was undeniably pleased at the peaceful end of one problem, but she was equally piqued by the way Jarrett was cuddling her against his side as if he had a perfect right to do so. Still, if she pulled away, the drunk was apt to be back in her face.

It wasn't until dessert was served that Jarrett moved, but even then he didn't release her entirely, just let his hand slip from her shoulder to the back of her chair. She could still feel the warmth of his arm. More incredibly, despite the click of silver and the low roar of voices, she could hear the whisper of his sleeve brushing against her shawl each time she took a breath.

At least, she thought, dinner was almost finished. With any luck, the speaker would be brief, and then the evening would be over.

They were just finishing dessert when Carl the concierge leaned over Kit's shoulder. "Sorry to interrupt," he said, "but I thought I should let you know that we're completely booked on the weekend you asked about. But the Westmoreland Room is open on the Saturday before that. Shall I book it for you, tentatively?"

Kit saw interest leap to life in Jarrett's eyes. "That's the fifteenth?" It didn't matter when she scheduled the auction, she told herself. Jarrett would never go along with the idea, so what difference did it make which Saturday night she chose? "I'll call you Monday to take care of all the formalities, Carl."

There was satisfaction in knowing that the first step

was in place. And perhaps it was just as well that Jarrett knew she'd rented a room. That would add to the impact.

She'd need a room on Monday evening, as well, she remembered, in order to carry out the next phase of her plan, but Carl had moved away as the waiters began collecting the dessert dishes. She couldn't ask him about it right now, anyway, without increasing Jarrett's curiosity. She'd just have to hope it wasn't a problem.

Kit turned to Jarrett with a smile. "About that date—"

"My dear! And you say you're not interested in me!"

"A calendar date, not a social one. Since it's your fund-raiser, and you said you'd fit it into your schedule—"

"Oh, I'll make it a point to be free. Do tell me what's going on."

Kit did her best to look innocent. "I'm still working out the fine points. But since you've boasted of being able to make any woman look like the sort in your ads—"

His eyebrows lifted. "Did I say that?"

"You certainly implied it. I think perhaps I'll sell raffle tickets, with the grand prize winner to be featured as your Lingerie Lady. At five dollars a chance—"

"Oh, make it ten," Jarrett drawled. "Then all you'll have to do to carry out your bargain by the fifteenth is sell five hundred tickets a week."

"And all *you'll* have to do is draw the winning name from a hat, make her beautiful and splash her photograph across national magazines using money you were going to spend anyway." Kit nodded as if in satisfaction. "Perfect fund-raiser. It should be a piece of cake, don't you think?"

"Oh, I can't wait to see how it all works out." Kit

gave him credit—there was only a touch of sarcasm in his voice.

"I'll call you as soon as I have all the details in place."

He reached into his breast pocket for a leather wallet and extracted a business card. "In that case," he said, "let me give you my private number. Call me anytime. I'll no doubt be sitting by the phone."

"Waiting to hear all my brilliant plans?"

He smiled, and she felt a bit bemused at the surge of pure energy that surrounded her. "Oh, no. I'll be busy figuring out how to fix the drawing so you win."

Kit's jaw dropped, and before she could think better of it, she sputtered, "But you can't—I can't—the rules..."

"I know. I'll have to work out how to get around that. But for right now I'm just thinking about what fun it will be to dress you for the photo session." He leaned back in his chair, head tilted, long fingers pressed against his cheek, surveying her. "Black, I think. Black velvet, perhaps. Unless you'd prefer white lace, with nothing underneath?"

CHAPTER FOUR

THE WESTMORELAND ROOM was considerably plainer than the Englin Hotel's ballroom, and on Monday afternoon, with the lights turned up bright, it was hardly the stuff of romance. But Kit wasn't worried about the atmosphere. Today, for the news conference she'd planned, the surroundings hardly mattered. And as for the bachelor auction itself—well, they'd just have to wait and see about that.

Privately, she was still placing her bets on Jarrett refusing to have anything to do with the event—though after Saturday night she was no longer quite so certain. The way he'd bantered about the raffle, without even pausing to think it over, had shaken her just a little.

Of course, it hadn't *all* been banter. He'd also managed to make it plain, without coming straight out and saying so, that if Kit went ahead with the raffle, he didn't intend to settle for the luck of the draw.

All the nonsense about fixing the contest so Kit's would be the name drawn out of the hat was only that, of course—nonsense. *In white lace,* she thought wryly, *I'd look like a walking stick wrapped in a fancy hankie— and he knows it.* No, he hadn't been serious about that. He'd used the image to make it clear that he wasn't above finagling the outcome till it suited him.

That was why the idea of the bachelor auction was so perfect, for he couldn't pull strings behind the scenes to control the results. The auction would be public, with every bid open to view and probably a healthy competition—maybe even rivalry—among the women who attended.

Kit supposed he could plant someone to bid on him, with orders to go to any financial heights so he wouldn't have to take his chances with an unpredictable crowd. But if he did anything of the sort, it would be very hard to hide. Tryad would be safe, because he'd never open his mouth about the auction again. If he did, nobody would take him seriously. And if he ended up paying thousands to get himself out of a date—well, Kit had never made any promises about precisely where the funds she intended to raise would come from. If Jarrett chose to dig into his own pocket to save himself the indignity of spending an evening with a woman he hadn't picked, that was his choice. It was all for a good cause, after all.

But even if he managed to arrange the results, she reflected, he'd still be on display. He'd have to stand in the front of the Westmoreland Room on a stage, under a half dozen white-hot spotlights, while a group of women debated his worth.

And that in itself, Kit thought happily, would be a triumph to be savored. Any man who put women on display as Jarrett did, month after month, deserved to be treated like an object. It would be fascinating to see his reaction to that—and Kit would be right up front watching.

Unless, of course, he did as she still expected he would and refused to take part. Which was why she'd arranged to make this the most public announcement of her career, so any objection or excuse Jarrett offered would have to be equally public.

Of course, now that it was far too late to back out, Kit would have given anything to be able to wander out of the room, down the grand staircase and away from the hotel to lose herself in the crowds on Michigan Avenue.

Not that she'd have to go so far to find a crowd. With five minutes to go till the official start of her press conference, there were already as many reporters milling around the Westmoreland Room as there were butterflies in Kit's stomach. Enough, in other words, to mount a major exhibit at the natural history museum. There were even a couple of video cameras from Chicago's most-watched television stations.

Kit was startled by the turnout. It must be a slow news day. She might get even better coverage than she'd hoped for. True, she'd called in all the favors she'd managed to accumulate—and more—in order to get these people here without giving a hint of what she was going to announce. In fact, she realized, she now owed more good turns to more people than she would be able to pay back in two lifetimes.

But despite all the trump cards she'd played, she hadn't expected so many people to show up. In fact, there was only one person she'd expected to be there who wasn't.

Did Jarrett suspect that the best way to mess up Kit's plans was to have nothing to do with them? Fortunately for her, she'd worked out a scenario that covered that eventuality, too.

Or hadn't he gotten her message? She'd called his private number this morning and told the icy-voiced secretary who'd answered that she'd like him to meet her for coffee at the Captain's Table, right off the Englin's main lobby, at five o'clock sharp. Then she'd bribed the maitre d' with a sizable tip to give Jarrett a note as soon as he arrived, directing him to the Westmoreland Room, instead.

But if he'd been busy all day and hadn't checked in

with the secretary... Or if he hadn't taken the message seriously...

The sweep second hand of her watch crossed the hour, and Kit took a deep breath, stepped to the podium and tapped the microphone. "Good evening, ladies and gentlemen, and thank you for coming. I'm Kit Deevers, of Tryad Public Relations. I have a short statement, and then I'll take a few questions." She glanced at the page that lay on the podium and cleared her throat.

"Domestic violence is an issue that concerns us all. As individuals we can't do much about the causes of that violence, but each one of us can help to repair the damages. We can help to provide shelter to women and children who have been abused. We can help them make a fresh start.

"Those things require money, and I'm here today to talk about a new, fun and exciting way for Chicago to raise money for the cause of domestic violence."

She raised her chin and looked over the room. "Jarrett?" she asked, deliberately letting her voice quiver. "Are you here? No? I'm afraid Mr. Webster has been delayed. At least, I hope he hasn't stood me up." She gave a nervous little chuckle.

Nobody in the room laughed. In fact, there was an uneasy silence, as if the reporters were embarrassed for her.

The things I'll do in a good cause, Kit thought. *Like letting myself look like an idiotic, helpless bit of fluff!*

She cleared her throat again. "He's authorized me, though, to tell you—"

There was a stir at the back of the room, and a tall, dark-haired man appeared, making his way easily and without hurry through the crowd. A smile here, a touch on the shoulder there, and within half a minute Jarrett was leaning on the podium beside her, looking earnestly into Kit's eyes. "Stand *you* up?" he asked. "I wouldn't dream of it."

His voice was husky, and she could imagine how it sounded, magnified by the microphone. She thought he'd probably planned it that way.

She gave him her best stunning smile and turned to the crowd. "I'm so glad he's here to give me moral support," she confided.

"My pleasure," Jarrett said.

Kit looked at her prepared statement again, trying to hide the satisfaction she was sure was twinkling in her eyes. This was better than she could have hoped. "Mr. Webster is known to all of you, I think, as the chief executive officer of Milady Lingerie and as a leader of Chicago society. I'm glad to announce that he's giving his time and his support to this wonderful cause by offering to be the grand prize in the very first Dream Dates Auction."

She didn't look at him. She didn't have to. He'd propped an arm on the podium next to her, and she felt his muscles stiffen.

"The lady who makes the largest donation at the auction will get to spend an entire weekend with Mr. Webster. He hasn't told me exactly what the weekend's activities will include, but I'm sure, with Mr. Webster's reputation, it will indeed be a dream date."

There was a spattering of surprised comment and some applause.

Don't let it go on too long, she told herself. *Let him get slapped in the face before he has a chance to think.*

She raised her voice and cut across the chatter. "Are there any questions for Mr. Webster?" She stepped back from the podium, her bright smile inviting him to take over.

The look he gave her promised reprisals later.

"What's the date?" a reporter called.

"Of the auction?" Jarrett said. "The fifteenth of this month. Twelve days from today, to be precise. Or do you mean the date I'm offering?" He shook his head. "Sorry, but Ms. Deevers won't let me tell you that. She says she doesn't know, but really she wants to keep it as a surprise so she can sell more tickets."

Kit's jaw dropped in reluctant admiration. The man was fast on his feet, that was sure.

"And I think she's being far too modest," he went on. "She's only talked about me. She hasn't told you a thing about all the other bachelors she's lined up to take part in this great cause. Perhaps you'd like to do that right now, Kit?"

He stepped back just a little, every line of his body an invitation for her to share the podium. Kit's feet felt as if they were mired in molasses.

"You *do* have others?" he asked gently. "Not just me?"

"Of course," Kit said. "I didn't want to take attention from your premier position. In fact, I'll be making announcements throughout the week, as more sign on—so, as they say, stay tuned. Thank you all very much for coming."

Chairs scraped. The noise level increased as reporters paused to chat to one another. A couple headed for the front of the room.

Jarrett cupped a hand over the microphone. "One would think you were anxious to get rid of all these nice people," he observed. "I wonder why."

Kit didn't answer.

"And you've cut your time even shorter, too. Are you eager to have all this behind you?"

"Of course not." Kit's voice was tart. "I'm having *such* a lot of fun."

"I must say I'm disappointed about giving up the raffle idea, though. The effort I wasted on turning a few scraps of black lace into a design suitable for you..."

She glared at him.

A smile tugged at the corner of Jarrett's mouth. "Kit, dear," he murmured, "where on earth did you get the idea that I'm not a good sport? Oh, yes—this *is* going to be fun."

Kit arrived at work early the next morning, but she didn't even get through the front door of Tryad's brownstone before she was greeted by a chorus. Alison leaped from the bottom step, waving a newspaper. "Are you crazy?" she almost shrieked. "A bachelor auction's bad enough, but dragging Jarrett Webster in on it, and making yourself look like a fool—"

From her perch on the marble-topped radiator in the little alcove near the door, Susannah asked, "Can't you think of a more interesting question than that, Ali? I want to know if you're planning to bid on him yourself, Kit."

"Why would I want him?" Kit closed the door and leaned against it.

"Why else would you set up this whole affair?"

"Because I'm an idiot," Kit said.

"You can say that again," Alison muttered. "Do you know what this makes Tryad look like?"

"A dating service?" Susannah asked brightly.

"No. That one was your idea."

"And it wasn't a bad one, either."

Alison ignored her. "What got into you, Kit?"

Kit took a deep breath. "I didn't have any choice about involving Jarrett. It's sort of a bet. I have to raise ten thousand dollars for his favorite charity—"

Susannah leaned forward. "Or what do you lose?"

"Has it occurred to you, Sue," Alison said tartly, "that we may not want to hear the answer to that question?"

"Speak for yourself. I'd like to know."

Alison ignored her. "What do you need Sue and me to do, Kit?"

Kit didn't realize how heavily the stress had been weighing on her until Alison's offer eased the load a fraction. "Bless you, Ali."

"Well, we're obviously all in this together."

More than you know, Kit thought. "The first thing I need is a date with Pierce. You don't mind, do you, Sue?"

Susannah's eyes widened.

"I mean, for the auction," Kit added hastily. "Do you think he'd agree? All he has to do is take the winning bidder to dinner or a show or something. In fact, I need every available man the three of us know—and I need them in a hurry."

Alison looked thoughtful. "Do you mean you went into that news conference last night and promised a bachelor auction with only one bachelor signed on? Kitty—"

"No," Kit said simply. "I went in without anybody. I didn't believe for a minute that Jarrett would agree to it."

"I think," Susannah said, "she's lost every last marble she ever had." She was apparently talking to the ceiling. "Alison's right."

"The difficulty," Alison pointed out, "is what we do about it now."

"Oh, that's simple. We pitch in and help make it a success." Susannah slid off the radiator and started up the stairs. "I'll go call Pierce right now."

The front door latch clicked. Rita was coming to work

right on time, Kit thought, moving away from the entrance so the secretary could open the door.

On the third step Susannah wheeled. "Unless—what *is* it you lose if you don't come up with the ten thousand bucks, Kit?"

Kit was the first to see that Rita wasn't alone. Behind her, filling the doorway, was Jarrett, tall and dark and elegantly turned out in a charcoal gray suit and the whitest shirt Kit had ever seen.

"Didn't she tell you?" he asked easily. "She's going to sleep with me."

"Oh, in that case," Susannah said brightly, "I *won't* call Pierce." With a swirl of her skirt, she disappeared up the stairs.

Alison shook her head. "I *said* I didn't want to know," she muttered as she retreated to her office.

Rita quietly went to her desk, put away her handbag, touched up her hair and turned on her computer.

Kit was left in the center of the entrance hall, face to face with Jarrett, who seemed quite content to stand quietly with one hand braced on the golden oak door frame and watch her.

"What are you doing here?" she said finally. "If you want to call a halt to this—"

"I'd have done it last night."

"No, you wouldn't. You'd have looked like a fool."

"Which was exactly what you were hoping for, wasn't it?"

Kit didn't answer.

"So now you're stuck with the bachelor auction."

She lifted her chin. "It's a great idea, and I'm looking forward to getting on with it. As you pointed out, I have only twelve days and a lot of things to do. So state your business and get out, so I can go to work. At least, I assume you have something to say? You didn't just cruise by so you could drop that bombshell about me sleeping with you?''

"That's what you call a bombshell?'' He shook his head sadly. "Kit, dear, I'm afraid you may be in for some surprises. I came to ask how I can help make this auction a success.''

"Oh, sure. As if you intended to do anything at all.''

His eyebrows drew together. "Why wouldn't I? After all, what's most important just now? I'd say it's that we raise all the money we can for a good cause.'' He sounded almost pious, but Kit didn't miss the sparkle in his eyes. "So I'm going to help in every way I can.''

"And commit a little sabotage on the side?''

"You're a suspicious sort, aren't you, Deevers?''

"You can't deny you'd like to see me lose.''

He paused as if to consider the question. "Well, there would be certain benefits to me—''

Kit felt her face begin to warm. *I will not dignify that crazy statement of his by commenting on it again,* she told herself.

"But I suppose it would be selfish of me to put my personal preferences ahead of the greater good.'' He nodded, as if he'd convinced himself of something critical. "So I'll pitch in and do my best.''

Right, Kit thought. *Like I'm going to believe him.* "I'll have to think about what you might be able to do,'' she said mildly. "Later, of course, when we have the program in order, you can make copies and fold and staple them. But for now—oh, I have it. I'll start you calling the list of grocers to ask if they'll donate snacks. That'll take a couple of days, at least, so come on up, and I'll find you a phone and the yellow pages and get you started.''

It was the first time she'd ever seen him come close

to losing his composure, and Kit had to exert all her self-control to keep her face straight.

Jarrett glanced at the gold Rolex on his wrist. "I'm afraid you misunderstood, Kit."

She feigned shock. "You didn't plan to plunge in right this minute?"

"I think I've mentioned next year's lingerie collections? I just realized I'm late for a meeting with my design team."

"Why am I not surprised?" Kit murmured. "Well, whenever you have a few minutes to volunteer, I'll be happy to see you. There'll be plenty of work for you."

That, she thought with satisfaction, *should keep him out of my hair for a day or two at least.*

"And just think," she said mildly. "It'll be a much greater satisfaction for you if you've given me every opportunity and all the help you can—and I blow it and fail anyway."

He grinned. "Exactly. You know, I am impressed by how clearly you see things, Kit." With a little bow, he pulled open the massive front door and was gone.

Kit took the stairs two at a time and shut the door of her office firmly behind her. She crossed the room in three strides and tugged two sharp-pointed darts from the big corkboard where she'd posted last month's Milady Lingerie ad.

Her first throw was slightly off, landing in Jarrett's left nostril. The second hit dead center, right between his eyes.

How clearly she saw things—indeed.

Unfortunately, the thing that was clearest to Kit was that the situation was only going to get worse.

The evening newspapers were even more wildly speculative about the Dream Dates Auction than the morning ones had been. Though Kit had long known that Jarrett was news in any context at all, she was stunned at the quick turn the talk had taken.

One of the society columnists had gone so far as to start calling Chicago's prominent bachelors to see who was involved. Most of them, to Kit's relief, had refused to answer either way instead of denying all knowledge of the auction. It seemed, Kit thought, as if they were waiting to see whether the Dream Dates affair was going to be the stylish event of the year or some crazy plan that no one with sense would take part in. It was obvious she'd have to move fast. She had to have something dramatic to announce, and soon—or the no comments would change into denials, and that would be death to the whole plan.

Susannah poked her head into Kit's office at the end of the day and caught her rereading the society column. "Maybe you should send that columnist a thank-you note for making out your list for you."

Kit didn't look up. "Having a list is one thing. But it's unbelievably difficult to get phone numbers for these guys, and as for getting through the secretaries…"

"Put Jarrett to work on it. He knows everybody, doesn't he?"

Kit said glumly, "As if he'd make an effort."

"Oh, that's right—he wants you to lose." Susannah settled herself on the corner of Kit's desk. "You could always offer to sleep with him regardless. Then he'd throw himself into the fray with enthusiasm, I'll bet." Her eyes narrowed. "Not funny? Sorry, Kitty."

Kit shrugged. *As if,* she thought, *with all the women in Jarrett's little black book, he'd go out of his way to sleep with me!*

"Well, at least you've got Pierce," Susannah went on cheerfully. "It's nothing fancy, I'm afraid. All I could dig out of him was lunch at the museum's restaurant and a guided tour of the new collections, but—''

Kit tossed her pencil aside. "That's what Pierce thinks is a dream date?"

"Well, it's typical bachelor behavior, don't you think? Not wanting to commit themselves to too much, particularly with women they don't know. I expect he thinks if he doesn't like the winner he can just prose on about Monet and Gauguin for a while, and she'll cut the whole thing short."

Kit sighed. "Thanks, Sue. It all helps. I've got one yes and three probables from my list, and two absolute noes."

"Who? I'll work on them, if it might do any good."

Kit tossed the list across the desk. "What I really need, though, is something dramatic, and a list of names isn't it. Neither is the sort of ordinary dinner-and-show sort of event most of these guys are willing to offer."

Susannah nodded. "Bachelors."

"Now if I could get someone to offer a Caribbean cruise, or a weekend in Las Vegas... I'd even jump at an event that wasn't exactly a date. Do we know any chefs who might offer to go to the winning lady's home and cook an intimate dinner for her and the man in her life?"

"Well, the fry cook at the restaurant around the corner might be able to handle breakfast in bed, but off the top of my head I can't think of anyone else."

Kit sighed.

Alison tapped on the open door and came in. "I suppose you've both spent the day searching out bachelors? I can't wait to see the bill you'll have run up by the end of this gig."

Kit decided she might as well bite the bullet. "There won't be one."

Alison's eyebrows climbed. "We're doing this for free?"

"I'll do as much as I can on my own time, and I'll make up the rest, Ali—"

Susannah slid off the desk and paced to the window. "There's a camera out there," she said suddenly. "On the sidewalk. And the man behind it is looking at our building."

Kit groaned.

Susannah waved at the cameraman. "Just think of the publicity we're getting, Ali."

"Thanks. I already have." Alison studied Kit for a long moment and said gruffly, "Just don't run yourself into the ground while you're trying to do it all, okay?"

Kit wanted to cry. Alison could be as blunt as a broken pencil, but she was also the warmest and most caring of women.

I couldn't ask for better partners, she thought. She pulled her list of eligible men across the desk and picked up the telephone once more.

Her threat to put Jarrett to work on the phones—the inspired strategy Kit had expected would make him run for the bushes and stay there—bought her just over twenty-four hours of peace. But at least, she thought philosophically when Rita told her who was on the telephone, he hadn't shown up in person.

"This is Kit," she said, nestling the phone under her chin.

She'd forgotten, in the few days since he'd called her from his car, how warmly intimate, how powerful his voice could be when there was no other impression of him to distract her attention. The deep tones resonated, almost tickling her ear.

"I've been racking my brain over this Dream Date

thing," he said. "And I wonder if you have any suggestions."

Kit almost dropped the phone. "Do you honestly expect me to fall for that line? I find it hard to believe that the king of lingerie, the creator of monthly fantasies, can't come up with a plan to entertain one woman for a single evening."

"You committed me for a weekend."

"So I did. Thanks for reminding me."

"It's not that I don't have any ideas," he began.

"I didn't think that was the problem."

"But everything I consider seems so tame. And I don't want to disappoint anyone."

"Me included, I presume?" Kit asked sweetly.

His voice dropped another few tones. "Can you possibly doubt the place you hold in my thoughts?"

Kit had to smile at that. He probably meant he cursed her every time the auction crossed his mind. "If you really want my input—"

"Of course I do."

"The first thing I'd suggest is that you stop thinking *weekend* and start thinking *week*—or even longer."

"Which will raise the price," Jarrett said. "That's brilliant, Kitten."

Kit had to grit her teeth to keep from snapping at him. If she reacted to the nickname, he'd probably never call her anything else. "Let's see. You've got that enormous sailboat—how about taking your dream date for a long trip to a deserted tropical island?"

He sounded a little doubtful. "How long a trip are we talking about? And do you think the bidders would really be interested in that sort of offer?"

"I imagine so. I know I'd like it immensely."

"You would?"

"Of course," she said demurely. "If I could afford it, I'd buy that package in a minute."

His voice warmed till Kit could almost feel equatorial sunshine spilling over her. "Standing on the deck of a boat with only the ocean for company... Fish, sun, waves, wind and..."

Kit moved in for the kill. "It's my idea of heaven on earth."

"Not bad, at that. Any particular island you'd like to see?"

"And what makes you think I was planning to go with you? It would be worth my money just to stand in the marina and wave goodbye. Some of those tropical islands are so far from civilization you couldn't even send me a telegram."

His laugh was a deep vibrato, which seemed to wrap her in merriment.

"Much less call on your cell phone to annoy me," Kit went on. "Now is there a point to this conversation, or can I go back to work?"

"Actually, yes, there is. I was talking to a few of my friends at the racquetball club this morning."

"And you recruited some volunteers?"

"Oh, no. Did you want me to do that, too, on top of entreating the grocers for donations? And what are you going to be doing in the meantime, if I'm lining up all the food and prizes?"

He sounded quite solicitous, Kit thought. "Never mind," she muttered.

"But I noticed an interesting phenomenon, and I thought you should know about it. The whole of Chicago seems to think the entire Dream Dates Auction is a publicity ploy."

"Can't think where they'd have got that idea," Kit said dryly.

"It's more than that, though. Every reporter I've run into—and even the guys at the racquetball club—seems to be expecting to start seeing us together."

"How charming of them." She was hardly listening.

"So shall we have dinner tonight? Or take in a basketball game?"

"No, thanks."

"Well, I suppose if you *want* to lose…"

Kit's jaw dropped. "What? Where'd you get that idea?"

"Because you're giving up a perfect opportunity for publicity. I'm just trying to help, Kit. If you don't want me…"

I don't, she wanted to say.

But there was no denying he was right. She ought to have seen for herself the potential for creating interest in the community by being seen in public with her star attraction, being available for comment and questions, taking every opportunity to drop bits of information to the media.

"All right," she said. "Make it the basketball game."

"I'll pick you up at the office at seven." He gave a sigh Kit thought was worthy of a lovelorn suitor. "I just hope we'll both be able to concentrate in the meantime."

"Hey, don't get the wrong idea, Webster," she said hastily. "I said I'd raise ten thousand dollars, and I'll do it, no matter what it takes. I don't plan to enjoy this."

"Of course you don't," he said gently. "But that's okay. It's all for a good cause—right?"

CHAPTER FIVE

KIT WAS adding another name to her list—a tentative yes who wanted to think about the prize package he would offer before committing himself to the Dream Dates Auction—when she heard Susannah's voice on the stairs. She glanced at the clock above her desk in surprise. It was past six, and she'd heard Susannah leave her office at least half an hour ago. Besides, who was she talking to? Alison was meeting with a client, and Rita had gone home long since.

"She certainly needs a break," Susannah said, and a moment later she put her head around the edge of Kit's office door. "Look what I found on the doorstep as I was leaving, Kitty."

"If you've brought in that photographer—" Kit bit her tongue a little too late and tried to change her expression to a smile. *All I need is to be pictured scowling on the front page,* she told herself.

But the man behind Susannah wasn't carrying a camera. In fact, Jarrett wasn't carrying anything at all, and he was wearing the most informal clothes she'd ever seen him in. His black leather jacket, half-zipped over a lightweight sweater, looked as soft as a cloud, and his jeans appeared to have been washed a thousand times, till they hugged his body with the same ease as his skin.

He probably pays a stand-in to wear his jeans till they're soft and comfortable enough to suit him, Kit thought.

"What photographer?" he asked.

"It's our first experience with a paparazzo,"

Susannah said. "He spent the afternoon camped out across the street. He's gone now, though. Poor guy—all those dull hours, and he misses out on the excitement, anyway."

"You mean Jarrett dropping by? I don't know that I'd call that *excitement*," Kit said. "And I'm sure I don't need to point out that you're early."

"I know, but considering how impatient you were to get out of the office last time we had an appointment..." He pulled a chair around and straddled it. "Thanks, Susannah."

"Never let it be said," Susannah murmured, "that I don't know a dismissal when I hear one. See you tomorrow, Kit."

Kit leaned back in her chair and tapped her pen on the desk blotter until she heard the front door close behind Susannah. "In fact," she added, "you're almost an hour early. Go away."

His voice was soft, almost confiding. "It occurred to me that though our date is for the basketball game, not dinner—"

"It's not a date, remember?"

He didn't seem to hear. "We do have to eat sometime. So—"

"I was planning to go around the corner to pick up a sandwich. You, of course, may do whatever you like."

"Then I'll join you. Lovely of you to invite me."

You're going to have to learn to be more careful about the way you phrase things, Kit told herself.

"Shall we go now?"

"No," Kit said perversely. "I'd planned to spend another half hour making calls." She swiveled her chair till her back was to him and dialed the next number on her list.

"All right. Walking into the game well into the first

quarter will probably get more attention than being there early, anyway.''

Kit frowned. ''Why? Won't everyone be watching the game?''

''No, they'll be wondering what we've been doing that was so important we missed the tip-off.'' Jarrett shrugged. ''But if you don't mind the comments, I certainly don't.''

Kit was torn between following through with her plan or giving up and admitting that he'd outmaneuvered her. Just as she decided to break the connection, the phone clicked in Kit's ear and a masculine voice said, ''Hello?''

Unable for the moment to remember who she'd called, Kit scrambled for her list and launched into her pitch.

Jarrett got up, pushed his chair into place and wandered across the room. Kit was momentarily relieved— he could have sat there watching her—until she saw from the corner of her eye that he'd discovered her dartboard.

The man on the other end of the phone line interrupted her halfway through her explanation. ''Is this the same silly thing Jarrett Webster's got himself into?''

''Yes, it is, though I assure you the cause we're raising funds for is a very serious problem, not silly at all. We'd love to have you—''

''Oh, why not? It might be fun to watch Chicago's finest make fools of themselves. Especially Jarrett.''

''I don't think you'll be disappointed,'' she said sweetly. ''I certainly plan to do my best where he's concerned.''

''Tell him I'll look forward to it.''

Another person who assumes Jarrett and I are seeing each other, Kit thought.

A few minutes later, she put the phone down, and Jarrett turned from the window. "Success?" he asked.

"Two more leads." She noted the details on her list. "And, for some lucky lady, an evening at the opera."

"Now that's a true dream date." He sounded almost admiring.

"Why?" Kit looked up. "I wouldn't have thought of you as an opera fan."

"I'm not. It's interesting you'd pick up on that fact, though. Is your intuition working overtime where I'm concerned, Kitten?"

How did I know? Kit asked herself, momentarily puzzled. She might be uncomfortably aware of the man's magnetic aura, but that was a far cry from being psychically tuned to his preferences. It must have been his invitation to the basketball game that had made his comment about the opera stand out in such stark contrast, she decided. Though of course nothing said a man *couldn't* like both....

And she was spending far too much time and effort thinking about what he might or might not like.

"Of course not," she said firmly. "Where you're concerned, I have hardly any intuition at all. But if you don't like opera, why would you think it's a wonderful date?"

"Because there's one outstanding thing about opera. It's utterly impossible to talk to your companion while all that caterwauling is going on."

Kit laughed. "And since the poor man can't choose his companion, at least he can control the conditions? Yes, I see why you'd think that was an advantage. Well, you'd better not postpone announcing your own package, because at this rate all the really good plans will be used up by the end of the week."

"As soon as I have it all figured out," he said earnestly, "you'll be the first to know."

Kit recognized the quotation. Her own words seemed to be coming back at her with annoying frequency. She also didn't miss the sparkle in Jarrett's eyes, which said he was hoping for a reaction, so she kept her voice deliberately level. "Just remember that the longer you wait, the more it will take to make a splash. You wouldn't want to look as if you were imitating somebody else's idea, would you?"

He looked thoughtful. "Only if it's a really good one."

"I've already given you a winner, Jarrett. It's not my fault if you don't take advantage of it."

"The sailboat?"

Kit nodded. "But I already have a trip to the beach and a day on a cabin cruiser on Lake Michigan. Yes, I think it'll take at least a month on a deserted island to compete."

"I'll keep that in mind," he said dryly. "Tell me again how much you said you'd be willing to pay?"

Jarrett's prediction was right—the game had already started when they arrived. Just as they came through the gate at the top of the arena and Kit got her first good view, the biggest star on the home team sank a three-point goal and the crowd screamed.

She clapped her hands over her ears as the roar swelled and echoed through the enormous space. "And you think *opera's* loud?"

Jarrett cupped a hand over his ear and bent his head toward her. "What did you say?"

His lips brushed ever so casually against her temple, and Kit jumped as if she'd collided with a high-voltage wire. Her foot landed in a puddle of spilled soda and slipped out from under her, and wildly she tried to regain her balance.

Instantly Jarrett's arm curved around her, warm and solid and supportive. "Careful! You never know whose lap you might end up in around here."

"Thanks," Kit managed to say. *Idiot,* she told herself. *You're acting as if he meant to kiss you!*

An electronic photo flash popped directly into her eyes, and Kit threw up her hand in a futile effort to ward off the harsh light. She tried to blink away the blue dots the flash had seared on her retinas, and cast a suspicious look at Jarrett. Had he spotted the photographer and planned that little stunt?

"I put my arm around you, and instantly you start seeing stars," he murmured. "How flattering, my dear."

Even with the game under way, the aisles were full of people coming and going to rest rooms and refreshment stands. In the confusion, Kit didn't object when Jarrett took her hand to lead the way down the steep incline toward the front of the section.

His reserved seats were at courtside, in the front row. No doubt, Kit thought, they were the best in the house. And no wonder he'd said that they'd get more attention by coming in late. With a momentary lull in the floor action, Kit felt as if every pair of eyes in the whole crowded auditorium was on her. Even a couple of the players seemed to be watching.

"Don't think I'm trying to influence you," Jarrett said gently. "But you might at least attempt to appear as if you're having a good time."

Kit wanted to thumb her nose at him. Instead, she turned to stare at him with enormously wide eyes and the most insincere smile in her repertoire. "Like this?"

"It might pass muster from a couple of miles away." He leaned back in his seat with the long fingers of one hand cupping his jaw while his other hand toyed with Kit's. "I hope you don't mind if I enjoy the game."

"Please do. I've never been much of a basketball fan, myself."

He turned to look squarely at her. "Then why did you choose the game over dinner?"

For the first time, Kit smiled at him with real warmth. "Because you didn't offer to take me to the opera," she murmured.

Jarrett burst out laughing.

The effect of that laugh, Kit thought in bemusement, was something like being dipped in a vat of warm, dark, sweet-scented chocolate. His deep, rich chuckle seemed to wrap around her, clinging closely and filling every pore till her body was steeped in his laughter, shutting out every other noise and sensation in the arena.

She swallowed hard. *It's only a laugh, for heaven's sake,* she told herself. *What's the matter with you?*

Still, she felt almost disappointed when he stopped, even though humor still lurked in his eyes and in the curve of his mouth. "In that case," Jarrett murmured, "I won't bother to explain the rules."

She refused to take the bait. "That's good, because I hate pretending to listen."

He settled to watch the game, and Kit turned her attention to the crowd, determined to ignore the fact that Jarrett was still holding her hand. Obviously, she told herself, he'd forgotten. He might as well have been toying with a soda can for all the attention he was paying to her.

It's probably an ingrained habit of his, she thought, *to hold whatever feminine hand is nearby.* Though she suspected the typical Lingerie Lady wouldn't be pleased at coming in a poor second to a basketball game.

While I, she told herself firmly, *am delighted.*

Despite herself, however, she found his enthusiasm about the game contagious, and she was soon caught up in the drama taking place on the court. As halftime approached she had even started to scream now and then. Once, after a particularly tense moment, she sank back in her seat, feeling wrung out, and caught Jarrett looking at her with a tiny frown between his brows.

"I thought you came to watch the game," she shouted.

"So did I," he said. At least, that was what she thought he said. It was hard to tell above the roar of the crowd.

Kit was feeling too hoarse to pursue the question, and in any case the action had picked up again. She said, "Sorry if my enthusiasm distracted you," and turned her attention to the floor, determined to be a little less flamboyant in the future.

At the halftime break, just as she was looking forward to a reduction in the noise level, a brass band took to the floor. Kit shook her head in disbelief. "It's a wonder anyone can hear after an evening of this," she said. "My ears are ringing."

Jarrett leaned closer. "Brace yourself. Here comes one of the vultures—otherwise known as Melinda Mason of the society pages."

Kit remembered the face from her news conference and from that evening's newspaper. Melinda Mason wasn't pretty, but she was certainly memorable, with her narrow triangular face and hard eyes. So this, she thought, was the woman who was calling up all of Chicago's bachelors to ask about the auction.

Kit drew a deep, sustaining breath, trying to make it as unobtrusive as possible.

Jarrett sprawled a little lower in his seat. "Hello, Melinda. I had no idea they'd shifted you to the sports beat. Are you enjoying the game?"

Melinda didn't bother to answer. "Is it true the two of you are involved in a serious relationship?"

"Oh, we're quite serious about the dream dates," Jarrett said easily.

"But not about each other?"

"Melinda." Jarrett sounded almost sad. "You can't expect me to answer that. If I say yes, I'm leaving myself open for a breach of promise suit if things don't work out. And if I say no, the lady here will be very upset with me."

"And no doubt she won't kiss you good-night," Melinda said.

Jarrett smiled at Kit. "Or something like that."

Kit had to admire him. Without saying a thing that he couldn't deny, he'd left the distinct impression that they were lovers. The man was as smooth as oiled steel.

Obviously the reporter agreed with Kit's opinion, for she gave a little snort. "Is tonight just a publicity stunt, then?"

"Oh, no," Jarrett said airily. "We're mixing work with pleasure. We're going to try to convince some of the team members to auction themselves off."

"You could just issue orders, I suppose." Melinda's eyes, colder than ever, turned to assess Kit. "And how do you feel about Mr. Webster offering a date?"

It was Jarrett who answered. "Oh, she thinks it's wonderful. In fact, she's planning to buy me, even if it costs a fortune."

"Is she, now?"

"The trouble is," he confided, "she wants me to offer a month in the South Seas—but I think she might be the only one interested in a trip like that. And if she was the only bidder she wouldn't have to pay a fortune, after all, and the cause would suffer."

Kit decided it was time to take a hand. "So would Jarrett. He can't stand the idea that he might go cheap."

"*Inexpensive*, darling. Nobody has ever accused me of being cheap."

The reporter sniffed and moved away. As soon as she was out of earshot, Kit said, "What did she mean, you could just issue orders? Do you own this team?"

"Only part of it," Jarrett said modestly.

Kit's heartbeat speeded up. "And you're serious about asking your players to be involved in the auction?"

"Of course I'm serious. I think at least half of them are eligible. Besides, why settle for raising a mere ten thousand when we could get into truly big money?"

Kit felt a bubble of excitement rising within her. With Jarrett throwing his support behind her—real support—the auction would be an incredible success. "Jarrett, that's wonderful! Now I'm really seeing stars."

"I thought you'd like the idea," he said mildly. "And just think how impressed I'll be with your skills when you manage to recruit all these guys without me even lifting a finger to help."

Jarrett kept up a steady stream of light comment all the way from the arena to Tryad. Finally Kit said coldly, "It seems to have escaped your notice that I'm not speaking to you."

"Oh, I noticed," he said cheerfully. "I just decided to ignore it. Same time tomorrow?"

"Are you joking?"

"You don't want my help?"

"This is what you call *help*? With one sentence to your head coach you could solve the whole problem, but will you?"

"Team manager."

"What?"

"The coach wouldn't go for the idea of the auction, but the manager might. And if I took over, it would violate the whole spirit of our agreement. It might even make me question whether you could have pulled it off alone, after all. Therefore, I believe I'll just stay out of it and let you prove yourself. Front door or back?"

"I beg your pardon?"

"Here we are," Jarrett said patiently. "At Tryad. I was just asking where you left your car. I wouldn't want you having to walk around the building at this hour of the night."

"What a gentleman you are." Kit's voice dripped sarcasm.

"Of course. I simply couldn't live with myself if anything happened to you."

She gave up. Jarrett had obviously been born with a better command of irony than she could acquire in a lifetime of effort. "Actually, I walked to work this morning."

"Which way?" He put the Porsche into gear.

"You don't have to deliver me. It's only a few blocks." But there wasn't much conviction in Kit's tone. The evening was cold and moonless, and she didn't feel enthusiastic about a stroll. "But if you insist—turn left at the stop sign, and then take a right a couple of blocks up."

A smile tugged at his mouth. "I thought you might see the advantages of letting me take you home."

"Well, don't get the idea that I'm planning to invite you in!"

"Isn't it funny," he mused, "the sort of thing that obviously came to your mind under the heading of advantages when I was only referring to taxi service."

Kit clenched her teeth hard and only released the pressure when it was necessary to give him further instructions.

The instant the Porsche drew up in front of her apartment house, Kit pushed her door open. She was standing on the sidewalk by the time Jarrett came around the car. He shut her door carefully and said, "You never did answer me, you know. Same time tomorrow? Maybe we can take in a male-strippers show."

She turned to face him and said sweetly, "Oh? Do you own them, too? Or do you simply enjoy that sort of entertainment?"

"Not at all." He sounded unperturbed. "But I'd put up with it for your sake in case you want to invite them to entertain at the auction." He waved two fingers in a casual salute and leaned against the car. "I'll wait here till you're safely inside."

He hadn't even touched her, much less carried through the sultry promise he'd implied to the reporter earlier that evening. And that, Kit reminded herself, was perfectly fine with her.

Of course she hadn't wanted him to kiss her!

The production room on the top floor of Tryad's brownstone was quiet except for the hum of the computer and the soft, rasping purr of the calico cat who lay across Kit's lap.

Kit put the finishing touches on a computer-graphic image and clicked on the button that sent it to the printer. As she moved to insert a sheet of paper, the cat opened her eyes and protested sleepily, then climbed from Kit's lap and plopped in the center of a puddle of sunshine to give her fur an indignant lick.

Kit leaned back in her chair to enjoy the peaceful surroundings. She loved this part of the public relations business, taking an amorphous idea and translating it into a solid form—in this case, a campaign to promote the new hot line number for reporting child abuse. If the board in charge of the hot line liked her design, it would go to the printer and then out to the public in the form of posters, radio and television spots and billboards.

Of course, the quietly technical side wasn't the only thing Kit liked about public relations. Working with people was fascinating, too. She liked to listen to them, to figure out the difference between what they thought they wanted and what they really needed. That, Kit had found, was the key to long-term client satisfaction.

Though why that should bring her thoughts to Jarrett as abruptly as a car smashing into a concrete wall was something she didn't understand. There was no mystery about what he wanted. He wanted to destroy Tryad, and more specifically Kit.

But why? The failure of the fashion show, of course—which he'd laid at her doorstep. What she didn't understand was why he'd chosen this way to take revenge. For one thing, why had he given her the warning and the challenge to make good instead of acting on his displeasure?

Wry humor stabbed through her. Maybe he'd been more impressed by her backward harem costume than she'd realized!

Susannah came in and spread the contents of a portfolio on a worktable nearby. "Will you be finished with the computer soon?"

Tugged back to reality, Kit sat up straight and reached into the printer tray for the finished graphic. "Right now, I think. Yes, it's all yours, as soon as I save my files."

"No big hurry. I want Alison's opinion, and yours, before I start. The paparazzo's here again, by the way." Susannah didn't look up from the papers she was sorting.

"I spotted him when I came back from lunch, lying in wait in the juniper bushes across the street."

"Sounds uncomfortable."

"It looked that way, too, so to cheer him up I told him what he missed out on last night."

"Sue—you didn't. Now we'll never get rid of him."

"Personally," Alison said from the doorway, "I think we should consider renaming the business."

"What?" Susannah sounded shocked. "You're the one who came up with Tryad, because you said Deevers, Miller and Novak didn't have quite the sound we wanted."

"Well, now I think Ringling Brothers and Barnum and Bailey would be closer to the mark. Not only did Kit make the papers again today, but in the sports section, not just the society pages. The phone's ringing off the wall, and Rita's tearing her hair out down there. She's taken five calls today from men who want to be included in the auction. She said to tell you she's keeping a list, Kit."

Kit snapped her fingers. "That's how I'll get rid of the paparazzo—I'll just go ask him for a dream date, and he'll probably take to his heels."

"I'm guessing he'll agree," Susannah said. "He seems a nice sort."

Alison grinned. "Then the question becomes whether anybody wants to bid on a day spent staked out in a juniper bush."

"It would certainly add variety to the auction," Kit said.

"And of course there's no accounting for taste." Alison moved across the room to look over Susannah's shoulder at the presentation she'd laid out on the table.

Rita appeared in the doorway, breathing a bit unsteadily after climbing two flights of stairs.

Or perhaps, Kit thought, Rita was nervous rather than short of breath—for behind the secretary loomed a uniformed messenger carrying a bulky package.

Kit frowned. No one but the partners were allowed in the production room. Not only was it more of a climb than most people wanted to make, but the presence of a client meant that pending projects for anyone else had to be concealed. It was easier to take materials downstairs to the conference room, or to clients' offices.

So why had Rita brought a messenger up?

"The package is for you, Kit," the secretary said. "And his orders are to deliver it to you personally."

Kit took the package reluctantly. Though it was big, it wasn't as heavy as it looked.

The messenger touched two fingers to his cap and departed as silently as he'd come. Rita hovered in the doorway.

"Maybe we'd better duck under the table, Ali, in case it blows up when she opens it," Susannah said brightly.

There was no return address, and Kit didn't recognize the handwriting on the label, though she had her suspicions—the ink was bold and black, the letters firm and upright and solid. It was not only a man's script, she thought, but the script of a man who was almighty sure of himself.

"If it does explode," she said, "just remember there's only one client lately who's been getting on my nerves—and vice versa."

"We'll engrave that on your tombstone if you like," Susannah offered.

Kit picked up an Exacto knife from the nearest drawing table and slit the heavy tape. Inside, wrapped in rigid foam packaging and more tape, was a large, unframed, full-length color photograph of Jarrett. He was wearing a tuxedo, and at the instant the shutter snapped, he'd been adjusting his bow tie and smiling at the camera.

And across the bottom corner, just above his signature, he'd written, *Isn't this a much better target for your dartboard?*

CHAPTER SIX

KIT SPENT almost twenty minutes constructing a message to leave with Jarrett's secretary—a message that was ultrapolite on the surface but would leave no doubt in Jarrett's mind about what she really meant. But when she called the number he'd given her, he answered the phone himself.

Kit was so disappointed she didn't bother to say hello. "What's the matter with your secretary?"

"Nothing, as far as I know. Shall I put her on the phone or just tell her you were asking about her health?"

Didn't the man ever miss a beat? "I figured, slave driver that you are, she must be having open-heart surgery, at least, in order to escape the telephone."

"I told you this is my private number. She only answers if I can't. You should feel honored, you know. Not many people get this kind of service."

"In that case, I'll start listing it in my biography under Honors Received," Kit murmured. "Thanks for the new dartboard cover, by the way." She leaned back in her chair and studied the board approvingly. The photograph fit nicely, with Jarrett's heart dead center on the bull's-eye.

"My pleasure. I couldn't help noticing that the other one was starting to look like Swiss cheese, and I'd hate for you to have to give up the game."

"Because if I don't take out my frustration on something inanimate I might start putting dart holes in you?"

"The possibility had occurred to me. Have you decided what we're doing tonight?"

"Well—no strippers, please."

"But how can you tell whether they'd be appropriate for the auction if you don't go see their act?"

"Oh, it isn't that," Kit assured him. "I just didn't want you to compare yourself to them and feel inadequate."

"Why do you think I would?" He sounded interested and not at all offended.

"Because you sent me a fully clothed picture. If you were truly confident, you'd probably have made it a swimsuit pose."

The silence that followed was brief but, Kit thought, telling. She thoroughly enjoyed it.

"Kitten, darling," he drawled, "if I'd only known you wanted one...."

"I don't. I was just saying—"

"But since you've asked, I'll look into getting one taken for you right away. In the meantime, I'm sure your imagination will be able to fill in the gaps quite adequately."

"You," Kit said with an acid edge to her voice, "need a swift kick in the ego, Webster." She hung up, cutting off his laugh.

And since she apparently wasn't going to be able to deliver the comedown he so desperately needed, she might as well quit trying.

Of course, she told herself, part of the trouble was that where the strippers were concerned he was absolutely correct. He *wouldn't* feel inadequate in comparison—not because of that all-consuming good opinion of himself but because, she suspected, he'd compare very well, indeed.

There was the way he'd caught her when she slipped at the basketball game, without showing the least sign of effort. And before that, at the fashion show, she'd fallen against him and ended up feeling absolutely weightless. There was no doubt the man was strong. The time he spent on his sailboat was evidence of that, and something he'd said about playing racquetball implied that it was a regular activity, not an occasional pastime.

And even though she'd never seen Jarrett less than fully clothed, there was something about the ease of his movements that spoke of strong muscles always warm and ready for action. Action of all kinds, whether it was sport or rescue or love...

Wait a minute, she thought. What was it he'd said about using her imagination? Just what kind of gaps was she trying to fill in, anyway?

In utter frustration, Kit threw every dart she could find at her new target. But even that didn't help.

Kit was packing up the sketches and examples of the design she'd present to the board of the child abuse hot line service when Alison tapped on her office door. "Can I talk to you sometime?" she asked. "I need a favor."

"Come on in. Just give me a couple of minutes while I finish this, all right? My presentation isn't till after the auction, thank heaven, but if I don't get my support materials organized while the idea's fresh in my mind, I'll probably forget half of what I need."

Alison perched on the very edge of the high-backed stool beside Kit's drawing board to wait.

It was funny, Kit thought, how different the three of them were. If Susannah was the one doing the waiting, she'd no doubt have flopped wrong-end-to on the chaise, propping her feet on the raised pillow section and letting her long blond hair spill over the foot. Kit would have probably paced. But Alison sat, hands folded atop a manila envelope on her lap, patient and still and ladylike as always—refusing to waste her energy on something that didn't deserve the effort.

Perhaps those differences helped to explain why they worked together so well, Kit thought. They balanced each other like a high-wire walker's pole.

She slid the last page of notes for her presentation into place, tied the portfolio's strings and put it safely into the side pocket of her briefcase. Then she tugged her office chair around till it faced the drawing board and said, "What's up, Ali?"

"Oh, it's this video script. Rita's typed the first draft, and I wondered if you'd have time to critique it before I run through it again."

"Is this the Windy City promotional film?" Kit held out a hand for the envelope.

Alison nodded. "You don't have to look at it right now, of course. I've got about three weeks before the production team meets for the first time, but if there are big changes—"

Kit nodded. "You'll want plenty of time to tackle the work." She riffled the pages. At first glance, it looked like Alison's usual careful and professional effort, but Kit was too experienced to believe that any project couldn't be improved. "Will it be all right if I get it back to you in a day or two?"

"That would be great. Thanks, Kit. This is a terribly important project for Tryad, and you have such a good eye for what doesn't work in video."

Kit laughed. "Too bad I don't have the same vision of what *does!* We could really use a specialist, you know. A production person with video experience." She sighed. "Maybe by the end of the year we'll be able to find the money to hire one."

Alison didn't comment. "Kitty, about the bachelor auction—"

"If you're worried about all the time I'm spending on it..."

"Not really. I'm worried about *you*, and how you're going to manage it all in such a short time. And so's Sue, only she's mainly concerned that you'll end up breaking your heart over Jarrett Webster."

"You could have fooled me. I thought she was trying to push me at him."

"She's trying to keep your sense of the ridiculous in focus."

"Well, if she has extra energy, I'd rather she help out with something that matters." Kit managed to smile. "It's going to work out fine, Ali. I'm in for another week of agony, but we're getting the kind of attention no firm could buy. And with all the new clients we'll end up with, maybe we can hire not only that production assistant but another secretary."

"We'll need them, if all those clients materialize," Alison said dryly. "Thanks for looking at the script. I hate asking you, when you're already overloaded."

"Paying work comes first," Kit said.

Alison paused in the doorway. "Want me to tell Susannah to lay off the jokes about you and Jarrett?"

Kit shrugged. "No, don't bother. She'd think it meant I was getting serious."

At two minutes after seven, when Jarrett's shadow fell across her desk, Kit didn't bother to look up. "You're late," she said crossly.

"Sorry to disappoint you."

"You didn't. Actually, you raised my hopes, because I thought perhaps you'd decided to give tonight a pass. But I should have known I couldn't be quite that lucky." She pushed her chair back from the desk and looked at him. Tonight there was no casual leather jacket. He was wearing a deep gray pinstripe suit, silvery silk shirt and maroon tie. He looked, she thought, as if he'd just stepped out of a boardroom.

"I could say I was making up for being early last night. In fact, however, I waited downstairs for a bit, but since there didn't seem to be an escort around I came on up."

"Susannah had a date, and it's Alison's night for volunteer work. And Rita, who's the only one who manages to keep regular hours around here, left at five."

Jarrett frowned. "Leaving the door unlocked?"

"It's a business office."

"But it's after business hours. This may be a nice neighborhood, but still—"

"How sweet of you to be concerned about my safety. Actually it's only been about ten minutes since Alison left."

The line between his brows didn't smooth out. "You could give me a key, so in the future—"

"Or I could leave the door locked, ignore the bell and the phone and leave you standing on the sidewalk. Now *there's* an idea!" She slid her list of bachelors into its folder and filed it in her desk drawer. "You'd better get busy on your dream date, you know, or all the celebrities who have volunteered will overshadow you."

"Celebrities?"

"Perhaps I should say well-known people. I'm not even having to hunt them down now. They're calling *me*."

"Congratulations." He sounded abstracted. Maybe even, she thought, a bit disappointed.

Kit tried, without much success, to hide her smile. She was going to enjoy listening to his apology when this was all over. "Yes, this auction is going to be the biggest event Chicago's seen in years," she mused. "Ticket sales are ahead of what I'd projected, and I've been asked to do a television interview. By the time it's done, Tryad will have clients standing three deep in line. What kind of dream date are you going to offer? At the rate I'm going, you'll have to come up with something wonderful to stay in the running as the star of the evening.''

"Maybe I won't specify what it is till after the bidding's over.''

Kit frowned. "And make it sort of a grab bag? Do you really believe the bidders would go for that? I mean, even for you, I don't think these women would put out big money without knowing what the prize is.''

"Kitten, you shock me. You're finally admitting that I have my attractions?''

Kit thought over what she'd said and found the unintentional compliment. "Don't get a big head about it,'' she recommended. "I can admit the average woman would find you attractive without actually feeling the sensation myself.''

He leaned against her desk, arms folded, and smiled at her. Kit would have sworn the floor rocked under her feet.

How perfectly silly, she told herself, to react that way. It was one thing to find him handsome and magnetic— no woman in her right mind would deny that. But she wasn't crazy enough to let that personal appeal of his knock her off balance, any more than she'd cuddle up with a cobra. So much for Susannah's concerns about her....

Still, she fiddled with her paper-clip dispenser for a moment so she didn't have to look at him, until the adrenaline rush had faded a bit and she was fairly sure her voice wouldn't crack. "Would you like to hear who I've snared just this afternoon? One of Chicago's aldermen *and* a minor rock star.''

"I'm duly impressed. Let's celebrate with dinner."

"Well, that would certainly be better than the strippers. Unless, of course, the opera is in town?"

Jarrett pulled her trench coat from the hook on the back of her office door. As he helped her into the Porsche, parked once more by the fireplug, Kit paused to wave at the bay window of the neighboring house. The corner of the lace curtain dropped hastily into place. "I wonder if the paparazzo realizes he's being staked out, too," she murmured. "Mrs. Holcomb probably knows every time he takes a breath."

"Is he back?"

"At the moment, he's under the juniper bushes across the street. I can just see the end of his telephoto lens. Shall we stop and tell him where we're going to dinner or make him try to tail us?"

Jarrett glanced at his watch. "Actually, I've got one quick stop to make first, if you don't mind."

"It's fine with me, as long as I can use your car phone while I'm waiting. I could probably convince a couple more people to join the fun if I tell them where I'm calling from."

"Oh, you're invited, too."

"Invited where?" Kit asked warily. "If it's some sort of formal occasion, I'm hardly prepared for it. Maybe I'd rather wait in the car."

The Porsche rolled to a smooth halt for a red light and Jarrett turned his head to study her. The leather seat cradled Kit comfortably, but it was so low-slung that it was impossible to keep her hemline in place. Her trench coat had fallen open and her narrow-cut skirt had ridden well up, and Kit had to fight the urge to tug it down to her knees. The last thing she wanted to do was let Jarrett guess that every instant his gaze rested on her raised her skin temperature by a full degree.

And just when, she asked herself, had that become a problem? *Get a grip, girl,* she told herself firmly.

"I really hate being a back-seat driver," she said finally, "but the light's turned green."

The Porsche slid through the intersection and up a ramp onto the freeway. "Actually," Jarrett murmured, "I was thinking you might feel a bit overdressed."

Kit waited a moment, but he didn't volunteer anything else, and she refused to gratify him by begging for information. How bad could it be, anyway? If, in her oatmeal-colored skirt and sweater, she was overdressed, then Jarrett was going to stick out like the Pope at a beach barbecue.

Still, Kit was startled when the Porsche turned in to the parking lot of one of the largest suburban shopping malls. "You need to buy some socks, I suppose? Or pick up your dry-cleaning?"

"Oh, no. It's a cocktail party."

"At the mall?"

Jarrett helped her out of the car and took her arm to guide her toward the entrance. "The Milady Lingerie store is showing some new fashions for its best customers, and I told the manager I'd pop in for a few minutes. You wouldn't want to miss that kind of excitement, would you?"

Kit pretended puzzlement. "I don't suppose that's a multiple choice question?"

The store was located on a prominent corner in the main section of the mall. Its single side window, discreetly draped with heavy beige-on-beige brocade, featured a mannequin wearing the scarlet satin teddy made famous by the current month's magazine ads.

"Nice," Kit conceded. "Rent the most visible location and then design the store so people have to come inside to get more than a peek. Plus the repetition when people see the same design in the window as in the ads must make the entire campaign even more effective. Is that the manager's idea or a chain-wide custom?''

Jarrett's eyebrows lifted. "Haven't you ever seen a Milady Lingerie store before?''

"Not a one. There are segments of the market you have yet to win over.''

"Then you're in for a treat.''

"I can't wait,'' Kit said dryly.

A discreet distance from the entrance, Kit spotted a half dozen women marching up and down carrying signs. *Sexist,* one of them said. *Unfair to women,* proclaimed another. *Milady Lingerie exploits females,* said a third.

She grinned. "Aren't you touched? A real live protest march—and all in your honor, no doubt.''

Jarrett glanced at the women and shrugged. "So?''

"Aren't you going to try to get them thrown out?''

"Why? It's a free country. They have a right to their say.''

Kit said thoughtfully, "It's also terrific—and free—publicity.''

A smile tugged at Jarrett's mouth. "That, too.''

"I see a camera coming right now, in fact. I don't suppose you hired them?''

"The camera crew or the demonstrators? Sorry to disappoint you, but I didn't think of either one.'' He pulled open the heavy walnut door and gave a little bow. "Welcome to my world.''

His world, Kit realized the moment she stepped across the threshold, wasn't quite what she'd expected.

She'd never given a thought to what the interior of a Milady Lingerie store would look like. If pressed, she'd probably have pictured red velvet and black feathers, rows of suggestive costumes and the heavy scent of perfume—the kind of atmosphere she'd expect to find behind the scenes at a bordello.

Instead, the atmosphere was closer to a drawing room than a boudoir. Gilded chairs, upholstered in the same heavy brocade as the draperies, were scattered in small groupings across carpet so lush and thick that Kit swore she was walking on a cloud. An Impressionist-style watercolor formed a focal point above a fireplace where a gas log blazed. The room was a sea of beige and cream and the palest of pink—shades that would flatter every woman, no matter what her hair color or the tone of her skin.

There were no racks of lingerie. There weren't even mannequins inside the store. Instead, a half-dozen models mingled with the customers, displaying with their every movement the luxurious sheen of satin robes, the soft rustle of silk slips, the glamour and glitz of lacy teddies.

Kit muttered, "No wonder you said I'd feel overdressed."

"The personal fitters are in the private rooms," Jarrett said. "If you see anything you'd like to try on—"

"Thanks anyway. Not tonight."

He grinned. "If you mean you'd rather wait till I can fit you myself—"

Kit glared at him.

"Jarrett!"

It was hard to believe that a single word in so soft a drawl could rake across Kit's nerves like a carpenter's rasp, but the voice was painfully familiar. Suddenly she was back in the reception hall after that fiasco of a fashion show, listening to Heather's mother calmly shifting the blame for the failure onto Kit's shoulders. Kit turned toward the woman, determined this time to face trouble head-on.

"My goodness," Colette said. "I thought sure the reports were mistaken."

"And it's nice to see you again, too," Kit said sweetly.

The woman looked Kit up and down and turned to Jarrett. "I hate to interfere in your business, Jarrett, but surely, if you wanted to do a fund-raiser, you could have hired any public relations firm in the city. Why would you settle for *her?* And a bachelor auction! Of all the silly, stupid ideas to come up with, that is absolutely—"

Kit interrupted. "You're coming, of course?"

"Are you joking?"

"That's too bad. I think you'd especially enjoy the swimsuit event."

Jarrett smothered a chuckle.

Kit let her eyes widen as she looked at him. "Oh, hadn't I told you about that? I'm serious, Jarrett. Swimsuit competitions are such a hit with the men who watch beauty pageants that I thought it'd be a nice touch for the auction, as well. And I think we'll have a tuxedo parade, too, before the main event begins, so all the bidders can judge for themselves what's available. After all, since beauty pageants feature a promenade of evening gowns, it's only fair if—"

Heather appeared beside her mother. Kit could hardly believe her eyes. The girl was wearing a duplicate of the scarlet satin teddy on display in the window. Despite her full figure, she looked particularly young and awkward in the too-sexy outfit. "Isn't this wonderful, Mother? Hello, Jarrett! I love your new line. I've tried on everything tonight, but this is still my favorite." She spun around dramatically.

"I'm delighted to know you're still young enough to enjoy dress-up games," Jarrett said calmly. "I'll make sure they save one at the warehouse, so someday when you grow up and can wear it for real, it'll be waiting for you."

Heather stuck out her lower lip. "That's very rude of you, Jarrett." She brightened suddenly. "Did you see the marchers outside making fools of themselves?"

"Heather," Colette said fondly. "Of course he saw them."

Heather ignored her mother. "Aren't they ludicrous? And a bit pathetic, too, especially the one with the sign saying, We Are Not Sex Objects." She laughed. "I'll say they're not! There isn't one of them who could wear this teddy properly."

"Neither can you." Jarrett's voice was cool. "So be a good child and quit trying to play Lingerie Lady, all right?"

Heather put her nose in the air, but she marched off toward the back of the store.

A model in a brief black costume swept up to Kit and handed her a makeup bag of the same beige brocade as the furnishings. "Here's a small gift just for coming tonight. Inside there are a number of samples and prizes, but there's also a gift certificate toward any Milady Lingerie merchandise, valid anytime in the next thirty days. It might be for ten dollars, it might be a hundred, but every lady is a winner."

"Thanks," Kit began, "but—"

"And if you use that certificate tonight, we'll add a bonus," the model went on. "So if there's anything you've been dreaming of, anything at all to please yourself or the man in your life..."

Colette said, under her breath, "Now that's what I call a waste of a perfectly good gift certificate."

The model glanced uncertainly at her, then at Kit, and when her gaze came to rest on Jarrett her smooth patter faltered for the first time. "On the other hand, I guess you *don't* need a gift certificate, do you? You're probably drowning in lace and satin.''

Kit tried to fight the warm blush that flooded her cheeks. She couldn't help sneaking a look at Jarrett. He was looking particularly angelic and agreeable, and she wanted to elbow him in the solar plexus—hard.

The model smiled uncertainly at Kit and fluttered on to greet a woman who'd just arrived. ''Hello, here's a small gift from Milady Lingerie for coming tonight....''

Colette sniffed. ''That girl is far too naive to be let loose on the world.''

Kit managed a smile. ''Not at all like your little Heather,'' she agreed. ''If you'll excuse me—''

Jarrett put out a hand. ''Where are you going?''

''Out into the mall to see if the demonstrators have an extra sign I can carry.''

He smiled at Colette. ''I think that means it's time to take her to dinner,'' he confided, and followed Kit out of the store.

The air of the open mall felt comfortably cool against Kit's face. She hadn't realized how warm the store had been. No doubt, she thought, they'd raised the thermostat so the models wouldn't turn blue. That way the customers wouldn't notice till after they'd made a purchase how inadequate silk and lace were for warding off goose bumps.

''The things women will do to impress men,'' she mused. ''They'll freeze, they'll squeeze into costumes as restricting as an Iron Maiden—'' She broke off to watch the protesters, who had lost a couple of sign bearers and were standing instead of marching. A security guard was keeping an eye on them from a discreet distance, and the camera crew had already left.

''Too bad,'' Kit said. ''If they'd done something really outrageous, the camera would still be there. Maybe

I should give them my card, since they could obviously use the guidance of a good PR firm.''

"That would be unethical," Jarrett pointed out. "You can't work for both sides."

"But you're not paying me, remember? So the rule doesn't apply. Besides, you'd get a publicity bounce from anything I did for them."

"Well, think it over for a day or two first, all right?" Jarrett took her arm. "Would you prefer French, Italian or all-American cuisine?"

"It doesn't much matter. I could eat a horse."

"That I might have to search for."

Kit wasn't paying attention. She was looking over her shoulder at the dispirited marchers. "If they'd gone after the issue of comfort instead of sexism, every woman in the mall would have at least considered joining in," she mused. "Underwires are the devil's invention."

"What?"

"It's true, and if you'd ever tried one next to your skin, you'd know."

Jarrett smiled. "Now that's an idea I hadn't ever thought of."

"Obviously. Men design lingerie for men, not for women."

"I beg your pardon?"

"For looks. I mean, of course, for men to look at. They're certainly not thinking of the comfort of women."

"I'll make a note of that. No underwires in your white lace affair."

"I thought you said it was going to be black. Anyway, it doesn't matter."

"Does that mean you'll wear either?"

"Don't bet on it."

"Speaking of bets, I've changed my mind about ours. About sleeping together, I mean."

"That wasn't a bet."

"Precisely."

"That was nothing more than a grandstand statement you made in order to—" Kit broke off and then asked warily, "What do you mean by *precisely*, Jarrett?"

"I mean it's not a bet. It's a certainty." He unlocked the passenger door of the Porsche and helped her in.

None too soon, Kit thought. Her knees felt like jelly that had just been spread on hot toast.

Jarrett leaned across her to solicitously fasten her seat belt. "However the auction comes out," he said, "you are going to sleep with me, you know."

CHAPTER SEVEN

KIT DIDN'T REGAIN command of her voice until the Porsche had swept out of the mall parking lot and onto the freeway. Even then, to her own ears she sounded almost pitifully feeble. "I think I'd like to go home."

"All right," Jarrett said equably. "Though I must admit I didn't think you'd be quite so eager. Just a few minutes ago you told me you were starving, and now——"

"I didn't say I was inviting you to come with me. And I'm certainly not going to bed with you, now or any other time."

"Now that's much more like you." He sounded almost admiring. "Defiance in the face of the facts—yes, that's classic Kit Deevers."

Kit's head was spinning, and she couldn't help wondering if he'd blown a gasket or she had. "I meant that if you're going to be ridiculous, I'd much rather be alone than with you."

"Oh, if that's what you're worried about, we should definitely have dinner. After all, I can't seduce you at a public restaurant. The maitre d' would object."

Kit closed her eyes. But trying to shut out the incredible only made things worse, she found, for with no outside stimuli, her imagination was free to roam.

You're going to sleep with me....

The words, soft and confident and assured, seemed to ooze through her veins like a hypnotic drug, washing away her resistance and leaving behind a sense of delicious lassitude. She could almost feel the stroking of fingertips soft as silk against her skin.

"And what's ridiculous about it, anyway?" The lazy tone of Jarrett's voice slipped into place in her fantasy as neatly as the right answer into a crossword puzzle, and for a moment Kit didn't realize he'd spoken aloud.

Then she sat up straight. "What's ridiculous? The whole idea, that's what! Why would you want to sleep with me? With all the models you've got running around, to say nothing of the Lingerie Ladies, who are probably delighted to have your attention—"

She had no idea what his answer would be, and too late, she found herself wishing she hadn't asked the question. Why had she been fool enough to phrase it in those terms, anyway? She'd practically made it sound as if she thought the offer was an honor. That was a long way from the truth, but still, she'd left herself wide open for a cutting reply. Did she really want to hear, in so many words, that he'd only been teasing? That he'd tossed the suggestion out in jest and was stunned at the strength of her reaction?

"That's part of it." His voice was so level, so sober, that there was no denying he was serious. "I wouldn't say that *every* model and Lingerie Lady wants my attention, but—"

"Don't even try for modesty, Webster. It doesn't become you."

"All right, I'll admit that a lot of them do. You, on the other hand, are a challenge."

"Gee, thanks." Kit sank into the deep leather seat. "I can't begin to tell you how terrific that makes me feel."

"Well, you did ask," Jarrett said reasonably. "And I thought if I gave you a pretty answer, you'd probably spit at me, so why not try the truth?"

Kit rolled her eyes and tried her best to ignore him.

"Yes," he mused. "*Definitely* a challenge."

Kit was tongue-tied. If she played along, she'd encourage him, but apparently even if she didn't play along, she'd encourage him. She was stuck in a lose-lose situation, and—judging by the upbeat tune he was whistling—Jarrett was enjoying it.

He pulled the Porsche up outside a row house at the edge of an upscale shopping district not far from Tryad's brownstone, and a valet leaped to attention and pulled Kit's door open. She shot a look at Jarrett. He didn't seem the sort to live in a row house, and certainly she wouldn't have expected an attendant waiting in the street. On the other hand, Jarrett was proving to be full of surprises tonight.

"Don't worry," he assured her. "It doesn't look like it from the outside, but this is absolutely the best French restaurant in greater Chicago."

Kit wasn't so sure it looked like a great restaurant from the inside, either. Beyond the maitre d's station, which was no more than a podium beside the front door, was a simple, almost square room containing a dozen widely spaced tables. Each was draped in snowy linen and set with elegant china and gleaming crystal, but only half were occupied at an hour when most of Chicago's restaurants were overflowing.

"Obviously an undiscovered treasure," Kit said wryly.

She hadn't dropped her voice quite far enough, for it was the maitre d' who answered. "We cater to a most discriminating clientele, ma'am—people who enjoy their privacy. If you'll follow me, please..."

Jarrett leaned close. "And that puts you properly in your place, I'd say." The laughter in his voice was like a fresh spring breeze stirring the tiniest hairs on the back of Kit's neck and sending a delicious chill all through her body.

The maitre d' led them to a small corner table and

bowed Kit into her chair. To her surprise, Jarrett made no move to seat her himself, or to pull his chair closer to hers. He took the seat opposite and asked if she would care for a drink.

"Yes, please," Kit said calmly. "Iced tea."

If she'd hoped to cause him an instant's shock or perhaps even a tinge of embarrassment by ordering something so plebeian, Kit was disappointed. Jarrett relayed her order to the waiter, asked for a Perrier for himself and smiled at her as he settled in his chair with the wine list. "I'm glad you agree with me that cocktails numb the taste buds and blur the entire experience of good dining."

To say nothing of blurring one's common sense, Kit thought. But saying so would tell him she was still thinking about that absurd announcement of his—which would be far, far better ignored. In fact, she told herself, she ought to have pretended from the very beginning that he'd said nothing at all. Or perhaps if she'd laughed in his face...

"I think, unless there's something you're particularly craving, that we'll let the chef surprise us," Jarrett said.

"That's fine with me. I seem to have lost my appetite, anyway."

A tiny smile tugged at the corner of Jarrett's mouth. "What a shame. I hope it wasn't anything I said?" He consulted the wine steward, and once the man had scurried away to the cellars, Jarrett leaned forward and tented his fingers under his chin. "I meant it, you know. You *are* a challenge. In fact, you're absolutely intriguing."

"Right," Kit said dryly. "So tell me, if you will, why someone who's such a catch would want to sleep with you?"

She thought it was a prizewinning question. If he answered it, he'd present himself as an egotistical fool—

almost a caricature of the breed—and she didn't think
he could carry that off with a straight face. If there was
one thing Jarrett wasn't lacking, it was a sense of the
ridiculous.

But even if he settled for a silent, modest shrug, he'd
end up looking conceited, a man so convinced of his
worth that no woman could possibly need an explanation
of why she should fall for him.

Kit was looking forward to seeing which he chose.

But Jarrett didn't even hesitate. "For the fun of it.
Because it would be fun, you know."

"As long as it lasted."

"Well, that goes without saying." The wine steward
returned with a dusty bottle, and Jarrett sniffed the cork
and sampled the vintage. After the steward was gone, he
cradled his glass in a lazy hand and nodded toward Kit's
untouched wine. "This really is good, you know."

"Of course it is. You obviously gave that choice more
thought than you did the offer you just made to me."

Jarrett winced. "I don't know why you bother with
darts, Kitten, when your tongue is even sharper. And
that's not true, anyway. I've been thinking about you
since—"

"Spare me the details, all right? And let's change the
subject, please."

"Certainly," Jarrett murmured. "I expect you'd like
to think it over. Just let me know when you've worked
it all out. In the meantime, I believe I'll set up an itin-
erary for that South Seas cruise, after all."

"Good," Kit said. "Maybe I'll be lucky, and you and
your dream date will run into a tribe of cannibals. Not
that I bear the poor woman any ill will, you understand,
but for the greater good of the world sometimes sacrifice
is necessary."

Jarrett smiled. "Oh, I don't mean for the auction. I'm

thinking about afterward—whenever you decide to come along.''

Jarrett kept his word about changing the subject. He talked easily about the newest fresh-from-Broadway play, commented on several recent best-sellers and elicited her opinions of the current conflict between factions of Chicago's city council.

He was not only well-informed but interested in her views, and although he didn't hesitate to disagree, he did so in a manner that was neither condescending nor judgmental. Kit was surprised. She'd expected him to be dogmatic about his opinions—or else, in an attempt to impress her, to fawn over hers. Either extreme would have been easier to dismiss than the reality, which was that she found him both refreshing and challenging—an expert verbal fencer.

And though he didn't bring up the subject of sleeping together, she could feel the question lurking under every remark, every gesture, every smile.

That perception was entirely her problem, and Kit freely admitted it. Jarrett was being a perfect gentleman. Still, by the end of the evening she felt as if she was walking on tissue paper stretched over an open pit. She couldn't clearly see the danger, though she knew it lurked under her feet. And she also knew that a single false step would send her plunging through.

By the time Jarrett parked the Porsche in front of Kit's apartment building, she was practically vibrating from the strain. She was relieved to reach home and eager to say good-night and escape. But instead of waiting beside the car till she was safely inside, as he had the night before, Jarrett fell into step beside her.

He didn't take her arm as they strolled up the walk. In fact, he'd hardly touched her all evening, nothing more than the accidental brush of his hand against hers as he filled her wine glass. But now, she could feel a sense of purpose about him.

I can't seduce you at a public restaurant, he'd said. But had his intentions changed now that they were in private? The fact that he hadn't harped on the subject didn't mean he'd dismissed it from his mind.

Just inside the main door, Kit turned to face him, chin raised, determined that if he so much as tried to kiss her—or, what she thought was more likely, if he suggested that he come upstairs—she'd slap him so hard he wouldn't see straight till next week.

Before she could speak, however, he'd pressed the button to summon the elevator and reached casually for her hand. "I've had a lovely evening, Kitten. Good night."

The brush of his lips against her lifeline was so soft it hardly counted as a touch, and so brief that Kit's brain hadn't yet reacted to the contact before it was over and he was gone.

"Fancy that," she said aloud. "The man can take a hint, after all." But deep in her mind was a hollow suspicion that he'd been laughing at her, as if he'd wanted to ask if she really believed he was so inexperienced a hunter as to rush his prey.

She pushed the button for her floor with far more force than was necessary and wished that it had been Jarrett's nose.

Her apartment was dark, and she almost tripped over the mail scattered across the carpet under the slot in the front door. She gathered up the envelopes and magazines and carried them into the kitchen, which smelled of the morning's leftover coffee grown stale in the pot. Kit washed it out and put in fresh grounds and water, ready for tomorrow.

She was tired, but far too restless for either sleep or concentration. She found herself wandering from one end of the small apartment to the other.

I can't seduce you at a public restaurant, he'd claimed. But in fact, she realized, that was exactly what he'd been doing—without a touch or a suggestive word, without so much as a gesture that any onlooker would have found questionable. He'd looked at her, and laughed with her, and questioned and charmed her—and by the end of the evening, she'd been almost disappointed when he'd kissed her hand and left her.

What am I thinking? Kit asked herself in shock. *I can't be so silly as to fall for that!*

She took a dozen deep and steadying breaths, and her confusion slowly began to dissipate. Yes, the man *was* charming. Deliberately and cold-bloodedly charming. And he couldn't possibly seduce her, in public or anywhere else, because she had far too much sense to allow it.

On that note, Kit went to bed, though she tossed uneasily for a long time before exhaustion overcame her. Once she was asleep, however, the palm Jarrett had caressed found its way to her cheek, and rested there.

And she smiled.

Kit climbed the stairs to the production room on Monday, carrying her lunch and a portfolio, and sat at the nearest light table. Susannah, who was at the computer, greeted her with little more than a grunt.

"Sounds like you're having fun." Kit found her chopsticks in the bottom of the bag.

"This darned logo," Susannah muttered. "It just won't work, no matter how I fiddle. What are you doing today?"

"Putting together the program cover for the Dream

Dates Auction. It has to be in the printers' hands by tonight if it's going to be finished in time.''

"It hasn't gone in yet? But the auction's on Saturday night.''

"Don't remind me.''

"Don't you have the program finalized?''

"Of course not. Rita's still getting calls, and there must be twenty bachelors still on my list that I haven't been able to reach.'' Kit dug into her rice and vegetables. "But once the covers are done, I can wing the rest. I want to delay as long as possible to have the most complete list of participants—so if I have to, I'll just photocopy the inside pages at the last minute.''

"Turn it over to Jarrett. He's probably got a dozen secretaries.'' Susannah frowned at the computer screen.

"That would be a sure route to disaster. He'd probably have them translate it into Swahili or put in every other page upside down—anything to make me look incompetent.''

"Really? Do you think he wants you to lose your bet that badly? You know, Kitty, you could just tell him the bet's off and you'll sleep with him no matter what.''

"Funny,'' Kit muttered. "That's exactly what he said. And no, I'm not idiot enough to do it. Thanks for the suggestion, anyway.''

"Then you're not serious about him?''

"What's to be serious about? The man's a Don Juan, Sue, and they always want what they can't have—right up till the moment after they get it, when they suddenly don't want it anymore.''

Susannah's face lightened. "I was worried about you getting hurt. But as long as you see through him—''

"Don't fret about that. I promise once this is over I'll be celebrating Jarrett's departure from my life—not mourning it.''

And the more deeply she engraved that truth on her heart, Kit reminded, the better off she'd be.

Susannah gave up on her logo and departed for a client meeting. With the cover finally finished, Kit gathered the refuse from the project and her lunch and went downstairs to her office. She'd make a few more calls and then run over to the printer's headquarters and get the program under way.

It's all going to fit together, she told herself. Before she knew it, the auction would have come and gone, the funds she'd promised would be doing good for Chicago's battered women, and she'd be free of Jarrett forever. And she was glad.

So why, she wondered as she pushed open her office door, was she having to persuade herself?

"Hello," Jarrett said lazily. "I was beginning to think you'd run away."

Well, that explains my confusion, Kit thought. *I was having a premonition, that's all.*

She stood in the doorway, eyeing him. He was stretched out on her chaise, his jacket draped over a nearby chair, his tie loose and the top button of his shirt undone. Frankly, she was amazed he hadn't kicked off his shoes. The calico cat was curled up at the foot of the chaise, her chin propped on Jarrett's silk-clad ankle. Kit couldn't quite decide which of them looked the more comfortable.

"What are you doing here?" she asked. "It's only the middle of the afternoon."

"I know, but I forgot to ask you about tonight. I'd hate to get here at seven and find you'd made another date in the meantime."

Kit tried not to smile. What a perfect excuse, and he'd handed it to her on a platter. "As a matter of fact..."

Jarrett interrupted. "So I checked your calendar, and

to my relief, it's empty. I thought perhaps we'd go to
the theater tonight for a change.''

"Because there's always such a nice social mix at
intermission, and you can introduce me to a whole lot
of eligible bachelors?''

"Well, I can't guarantee how many will be seeing a
fresh-from-Broadway extravaganza on a Monday night,
but—''

"I didn't think so.'' She dumped the remains of her
lunch in the wastebasket beside her desk and laid the
finished program cover on the blotter, right next to her
calendar and atop the list of bachelors who'd committed
to offering dream dates.

The all-important bachelor list—which she'd care-
lessly left lying there, open to view. It seemed undis-
turbed, but Jarrett couldn't have missed it. In fact, he'd
probably found it just as exciting a read as the best-
sellers he'd talked of last night over dinner.

She wondered if that was why he seemed so relaxed.
Or perhaps he'd still been studying it when he heard her
step outside the office and he'd flung himself on the
chaise to pretend an ease he didn't feel.

The question wasn't whether he'd read it, that was
sure. It was what, if anything, he intended to do with
the information. Would he call everyone on her list and
suggest that they didn't want to be involved in the auction, after all?

She'd find out soon enough, Kit supposed. If her
dream dates began to collapse like falling dominoes...
Well, she'd deal with that when and if it happened.

"Who let you in, anyway?'' she asked. "Nobody's
supposed to be in any of the offices without a partner
present.''

"Nobody,'' he admitted. "I just waved at Rita, because she was on the telephone, and came on up. You

know, Kitten, I've been thinking about it, and you're right.''

The man was like quicksilver, she thought warily. She could think of a half dozen subjects he might be referring to, and the only thing she was certain of was—whatever the subject—he was up to no good. ''I'm right about what?''

''Needing volunteers. So here I am.'' He sat up, arms outstretched as if to embrace the job. ''I've told my secretary not to count on me being in the office for the rest of the week so I can devote myself to you.''

''Oh, joy,'' Kit said faintly.

Jarrett grinned. ''I knew you'd be thrilled. I've already started, in fact.''

Kit wasn't sure she wanted to know what he meant, but she asked anyway. ''With what?''

''Rita put a call through a few minutes ago, and—''

''Rita let you talk to one of my clients?''

Jarrett shook his head sadly. ''There's no need to shout, Kitten. And you don't have to go storming downstairs and fire her, either. Of course she didn't let me talk to a client.''

Kit's heart started to beat again. ''Then who?''

''It was only the concierge person at the Englin Hotel. The one you were talking to at the banquet that night.''

''Carl? What did he want?''

''He was phoning to tell you they've had a cancellation the night of the auction. Something about a wedding coming apart at the seams.''

''What's that got to do with the auction?''

''He wondered if we'd like to have the ballroom instead, since it's available now. I told him we would.''

We, Kit thought, almost amused. He'd gone from volunteer to decision maker in record time. Then the importance of what he'd said hit her like a rock slide.

"Jarrett—" Her voice was little more than a squeak, and she had to stop and clear her throat. "You've been in that ballroom. You know perfectly well it holds two thousand people. The Westmoreland Room holds two hundred, tops."

"Yes. That's the beauty of it. We'll be able to make twenty times as much money on the tickets alone."

"But only if we sell twenty times the tickets. If we don't, the place will look like a ghost town."

He shook his head sadly. "I worry about you sometimes, Kitten. Such a lack of self-confidence."

"Can't you see I'm just being realistic? Two hundred people in the Westmoreland Room will be seen as an overwhelming success. Put the same two hundred in that enormous ballroom, and everyone in town will be talking about what a shame it is the auction fell flat. Dammit, Jarrett—" She paused. Talking to him was going to get her nowhere. She reached for the telephone.

"But I thought you were certain of success. You did say ticket sales were running ahead of what you'd hoped, didn't you?"

"Not *that* far ahead."

"Who are you calling, by the way?"

"Carl, so I can tell him the auction will be in the Westmoreland Room as originally planned."

"Oh, didn't I tell you?"

The faux innocence in his voice made Kit consider hitting him over the head with the phone. "Tell me what?"

"The main reason he called to ask about shifting the auction. Somebody else wants to rent the Westmoreland Room that night."

Kit put the phone down and slowly sank into her chair.

"Good," Jarrett said. "I'm glad you're finally relaxing. It's no easier to seduce you sitting than standing, you know—you're perfectly safe to sit down in my presence.''

This is not relaxing, she thought. *This is a state of total nervous collapse.*

But admitting that he'd so neatly boxed her into a corner would only gratify him, and she'd be darned if she'd give him any extra reason to feel triumphant.

''With two thousand people,'' she said grimly, ''we'll need a lot more hors d'oeuvres. Which means, as soon as you finish the list of nearby grocers and food distributors, you can start on the suburban supermarkets and ask them to donate, too.''

Though it was the best shot in her armory at the moment, she wasn't surprised when Jarrett shrugged it off. ''Toss me the phone book. And by the way, I brought you something.''

''Another gift? I'm sorry, but I only have one dartboard.''

''Oh, it's not the swimsuit photo. That will take another week, at least.'' He reached behind the chaise and handed her a flat rectangular box, about the size that would hold a dress, wrapped in heavy paper that looked exactly like the brocade draperies in the windows of Milady Lingerie.

Which was a dead giveaway of where it had come from, Kit thought with a touch of foreboding.

She kept her voice deliberately casual. There was no sense in overreacting. The fact that he gave her something certainly didn't mean she had to wear it. ''This is the white lace something, I suppose?'' She tugged the cream-colored ribbons loose and slid a fingernail under the strip of tape that held the paper tight.

Jarrett frowned. ''I thought you'd decided on black. In any case, no, it's not that.''

Kit's hand slipped. *Oh, great,* she thought. *Now what's he come up with?* "You mean you haven't finished it? What kind of a designer are you, anyway, taking all this time?"

"Oh, my part's finished. But I had to special order flesh-colored tissue paper so you could stuff it properly, and that hasn't arrived yet."

She picked up the closest object, a glass paperweight that Alison had given her last Christmas, and threw it at him.

He fielded it expertly. "Nice pitch, Deevers. You can join my baseball team anytime you want."

Kit warily lifted the lid off the box, as if the contents were hissing. Inside, wrapped in more satiny paper, she could see a gleam of sapphire blue.

"I should warn you, it didn't come from Milady. I only had it wrapped there."

"Why doesn't that comfort me?" Kit muttered. She pulled the paper loose to reveal the chiffon harem outfit she'd modeled at the debs' fashion show—the ensemble she'd been wearing when she first saw him.

"Just a little remembrance of a special occasion," he said modestly. "Besides, it's exactly the color of your eyes."

"If you try to tell me that you noticed *that* at the fashion show—"

"But I did," he protested. "Right along with your magnificent shoulder blades."

"You enjoyed that display, didn't you?" She put the lid on the box. "And now the costume's all mine, so I can do as I like with it—right?"

"Of course."

"Good. I'll make sure to pass it on to whichever lady bids highest for you."

He thoughtfully rubbed his jaw. "So that whenever I

look at her, I'll think of you? Kitten, I had no idea you possessed such a romantic soul!''

"The next thing I throw at you,'' she warned, "will be heavier and harder to catch.''

"Yourself?''

She picked up her dictionary and hefted it experimentally.

"Excuse me,'' Jarrett said quickly, "but I really do have work to do. Where's that list of grocers?''

He reached for the telephone book. Then he pulled the stool away from her drawing board and toward the corner of her desk, setting it right next to her chair.

Another deliberate maneuver, Kit told herself, *which will be best ignored.*

Dismissing him from her mind was easier said than done, however. Her senses were atingle with his nearness. A hint of his cologne wafted through the air to tickle her nose, the warmth of his body seemed to reach out to her, the soft rustle of his shirt was almost a whisper in her ear. From the corner of her eye, she could see the way his soft, dark hair curved around his ear, and the fine pores of his skin.

"You know, Kitten,'' he said suddenly.

Kit jumped as if an ice cube had been slipped down her back.

"What you said a little while ago about throwing yourself at me—''

Automatically, she defended herself. "I didn't say anything like that. You jumped to conclusions.''

He said plaintively, "You are the most contrary woman I've ever met.''

"I thought that's what you liked about me.''

"Oh, it is. Nevertheless—''

"So maybe,'' Kit said thoughtfully, "if my main attraction for you is that I *don't* want to sleep with you—''

"I wouldn't go quite that far," he mused. "But do go on. You were saying?"

"Then if I pretend to be eager, you'll lose interest?"

Jarrett's eyes brightened. "I don't know. Shall we try it and find out?"

"How about if I think it over and let you know?"

"Cold feet, Kitten?" he chided. "I never thought you'd be afraid to take a risk."

He went back to his list, and Kit stared at her desk blotter.

The trouble was, she realized, he was right. She *was* afraid. Not of him, but of herself. If she let down her guard for an instant, the attraction she couldn't deny feeling for him would overwhelm her like a tsunami.

And if that happened, she was terrified that the pleasure he offered—the fun he had promised an affair with him would be—might just seem worth the risk.

CHAPTER EIGHT

SHE WAS CRAZY even to consider the possibility of having an affair with him, and Kit knew it. But recognizing the insanity didn't make it go away.

She had honestly had no idea, until that moment of realization, how deeply she had let herself become mired in thinking about and reacting to Jarrett.

The attraction she felt was perfectly understandable, of course. Jarrett was a force to be reckoned with, a masculine presence any woman was apt to find as heady as the best vintage of the century. And since Kit had been thrown into closer contact with him than most women had the opportunity to experience, it was no wonder she was feeling the effects.

Now that she'd paused to think it over, Kit could see exactly where she'd made her mistake. She'd taken a wrong turn clear back at the beginning. She'd assumed that because her first encounters with him had given her a bad reaction, she would continue to be immune to his charm.

But it hadn't worked out that way. The vaccination hadn't taken, and now she was suffering the consequences—which were threatening to be as messy and inconvenient as a flu virus.

She wanted to put her head on her desk blotter and cry in frustration. Instead, she sat up straighter and tried to ignore him.

The only sound she could hear was the scratch of Jarrett's fountain pen against the fibers of the notepad on which he was writing some kind of list. From the very corner of her eye, she couldn't read the words, but each was neat and almost elegant, laid out by a fine gold nib in coal-black ink against the yellow paper.

His pen resembled green marble, but he held it not like cold stone but as if it was a warm and living extension of his hand. He wielded the instrument with easy grace, almost as if it was a sensual pleasure—with just enough pressure to achieve the desired result. Just as he no doubt would caress a lover's skin...

Great job you're doing of ignoring him, Deevers, she told herself tartly. *Why not just go hang yourself right now and have it over with?*

"Kitty!" Susannah's panicked voice echoed down the stairs. "Are you down there? The computer ate my logo! Please come and make the damned thing give it back!"

Jarrett lifted the nib of his pen from the paper and gave Kit a quizzical look.

She shrugged. "Alison's the practical one, Susannah's the visionary, I'm the technician. When the computer needs discipline, they both scream for me."

His voice was full of lazy humor. "And Kitten rides to the rescue?"

Not quite, Kit wanted to say. *In this case, it's Susannah who's doing the rescuing.*

The air that stirred in the hallway as Kit passed through felt cool against her face. She hadn't realized how warm her office was. Apparently, another of Jarrett's talents was being able to raise room temperature faster than a half dozen halogen lamps.

Susannah was standing beside the computer station, staring unbelievingly at an absolutely black screen. *Not a good sign,* Kit thought, but she tried to keep her voice light. "I haven't seen a monitor that looks like that one since they invented screen savers. And even then it was in a museum."

Susannah closed her eyes and put both hands to her temples.

"I'm sure you've already tried all the obvious fixes?"

Susannah nodded. "At least three times each," she said drearily. "With no results. What did I do? Crash the whole thing?"

"Oh, no. The monitor may have blown, but the computer sounds fine, so all your data is probably still there. It's just that without being able to see what we're doing... You did save it, didn't you?"

"Only the first version. Not the changes I'd just made."

Kit sighed. "Well, I'm afraid they're history." A half dozen keystrokes later, she leaned back in her chair. "Hey, Sue. You can open your eyes now."

Cautiously, Susannah did, and sighed in relief when she saw her logo once again displayed. "Then I *didn't* blow it up?"

"You didn't even lose your most recent work."

"Kit, you darling—I owe you anything you want. Name it."

"I'll remember that. But I didn't do much, really."

"I don't care—it feels like plenty." Susannah sat at the keyboard again, and Kit went downstairs.

The break had served, like a fresh breeze, to clear her head and restore her sense of balance. She'd be all right now.

The whole experience of finding herself actually attracted to the man had probably been fortunate, she told herself. Shocking as the realization had been, it was better to know what was going on than to continue naively down a path that would lead only to trouble. She was lucky to see the truth while there was still time to draw back.

Now that she knew what she was dealing with, she

was no longer in any real danger of falling for the man. She'd treat this incredible crush on him just as she would a head cold—an unpleasant but not life-threatening condition that would soon run its course and be nothing but memory.

She was smiling as she reached her office. The idea of Jarrett being no more important than a head cold—now that was an image she could cherish!

Jarrett was still sitting beside her desk, but the fountain pen and the notepad were no longer in sight. He'd slouched in his chair and propped his feet on her desk blotter with his ankles crossed. In one hand he held a small plastic bottle, in the other a wand—part of the treasures Susannah had tucked in her Christmas stocking last year. As Kit stared in utter disbelief he raised the wand to his lips, blew gently and tipped his head to watch as an enormous and iridescent bubble rose effortlessly toward the ceiling.

Kit swallowed hard. She had never before encountered a man so magnetic, so intensely fascinating, so secure in himself that he could sit with his feet up and blow bubbles without threatening his masculinity in the least.

The bubble shattered. In the quiet room, Kit heard the soft pop as clearly as if it had been an explosion. Or perhaps it wasn't the bubble's demise she heard, but the end of her illusion that mere knowledge could protect her from his charms.

Jarrett looked up and smiled, and Kit's heart squeezed painfully tight.

"Hi," he said. "Was the resuscitation effort a success?"

"Susannah's breathing again, at least."

"That's good. I like her."

Jealousy stabbed through Kit like a javelin. The reaction stunned her. He'd only been making a casual comment—hadn't he? Besides, she couldn't possibly feel jealous over a man she didn't really want—could she? And jealous of Susannah? Her friend, her partner—a woman who was almost as close as a sister?

"I hope you don't mind the bubbles," Jarrett said. "I'm trying not to let them hit anything important."

"That's good. Soap rings don't look good on presentation packages." Kit's voice was incredibly steady, considering what was going on in her mind. "I thought you were calling grocers. Or are you already through the list?"

"I decided it was far too much effort."

She was momentarily nonplussed, but finally she shrugged. "All right. The night of the auction, I'll tell two thousand hungry people to blame you."

"Oh, they'll be fed. I just decided it was pointless to waste time soliciting small donations from every grocer in the city, so I called a restaurateur friend. He's taking over the whole thing. Hors d'oeuvres for two thousand, coming right up."

"And who gets the bill?" she asked doubtfully.

"He's donating it."

"The whole thing?"

Jarrett nodded and blew another bubble. This one drifted off to the side and burst against the shade of her desk lamp.

"That's some friend. Either he's extremely generous or he's planning to do it on the cheap. What's he going to bring? Cheese cubes and saltines?"

"He didn't say."

She rubbed the back of her neck. She didn't manage to ease the tense muscles, but she did loosen her French twist. "Well, it probably doesn't matter," she mused. "The auction will be the main thing. At least we're not promising a sit-down dinner."

Jarrett put the soap solution aside and sat up straight. "You know, that's not a half-bad idea. A dinner would—"

Kit glared at him. "Let me make this perfectly clear, Webster. Your involvement in food is over. Nothing more—do you understand?"

"Yes, ma'am." Both his words and his tone were meek.

Kit wasn't fooled for an instant. The busier she kept him, the better off she'd be. "So since you've finished that assignment, you can go to work on ticket sales."

"Me? But Kitten, darling, you're doing such a good job. I couldn't bear to interfere. Of course," he added thoughtfully, "if you don't get two thousand people there, you'll end up with a whole lot of cheese on your face. By the time you eat it all, you'll probably have grown whiskers." He reached out a casual hand. "You'd make a cute sort of mouse. But we'd absolutely have to change your name."

With the tip of his smallest finger, he traced imaginary lines on her cheeks, just where a mouse would have whiskers. Kit wanted to stand still and let him finish, just to prove that his little trick had no effect on her. But that wasn't true. Though his touch was soft as a feather, the slow, deliberate stroking was enough to drive her mad.

She couldn't take it any more. She stepped back, just out of reach, with more speed and less grace than she'd have liked.

Jarrett smiled.

Kit wanted to stamp on his foot. But this sort of provocation, she told herself, called for far more definite action than that.

Maybe, she thought, she'd been onto something earlier, after all. If she stopped playing hard to get, he'd probably back off, concerned about the consequences of his actions.

What she ought to do, she realized, was throw herself into his arms and give him a hot and passionate kiss. That might just terrify him into cutting out this kind of nonsense....

But the very thought made her dizzy. She could actually feel the strength of his body held close in her arms. She could hear the beat of his heart—or was it her own? She could feel the texture of his skin against her fingertips and taste his lips against hers....

Kit's head was spinning, and she had to clutch at the back of a chair to keep herself upright.

No, she thought, there were too many ways to interpret a kiss, and Jarrett was guaranteed to seize on the one he wanted—that she'd agreed to an affair. While she was convinced he'd soon tire of the whole idea if she was no longer a challenge, it was likely to take a while—and if a kiss that had occurred only in her imagination could send her blood pressure through the roof, Kit knew she'd better stop cherishing any illusions about how much she could stand in real life.

But perhaps there was a better idea. What would happen if she seemed to be getting *serious* about him?

That was the answer, she realized. The moment she hinted that she expected—counted on—something more long-lasting than an affair, Jarrett would be no more than a streak of dust in the distance.

She realized abruptly that Jarrett's hand was inches from her face and that he'd snapped his fingers under her nose at least twice. "Are you all right?" he asked.

Kit smiled. All of a sudden, she was feeling much more sure of herself. "Never better," she said.

He looked a bit wary, she thought. This would require careful handling. "Let's get some work done." She dug in her desk drawer for a folder. "Here's a list of the ticket outlets. If we're trying to fill the ballroom, I'll have to get another batch of tickets printed. And some extra promotion wouldn't hurt."

Jarrett ran an eye down the list. "What have you got in mind?"

"I think I told you I'm scheduled on one of the TV talk shows tomorrow morning. I was going to make the appearance by myself, but two of us would be even better. And since you're going to be available the rest of the week..." She held her breath.

But Jarrett didn't even hesitate. "Sure," he said. "Good idea."

Kit cupped her hand over the side of her face as she looked at her folder. But she wasn't studying the list of ticket outlets. She was trying to hide the smile she couldn't quite repress.

This, she thought, *might actually end up being fun.*

When Kit's doorbell rang on Tuesday morning, dawn was no more than a faint promise in the eastern sky. She was still drinking her first cup of coffee and trying to decide whether fake pearls or a twisted rope of gold would look better under the pitiless glare of television lights. She gave up the question and pulled the door open without bothering to secure the chain. "It's bad enough of you to make a habit of being early," she grumbled, "but at this hour of the morning it's positively indecent."

Jarrett shrugged. "If you'd only taken me up on the idea of sleeping together, you could have spent the night at my place. And since my apartment happens to be just a few blocks from the television station, neither of us would have had to get up at such a ghastly hour."

It really wasn't fair, Kit thought wryly, that he was

not only early, but wide awake into the bargain. "Well, the part about *sleeping* isn't a bad idea."

"Poor Kitten." He sounded quite solicitous. "Aren't you resting well these days?"

Kit didn't bother to dignify that with a comment, figuring that he could perfectly well judge for himself. Jarrett, in contrast, looked as if he'd not only had a full night's sleep but had just stepped out of his tailor's shop. His topcoat was open over a trimly tailored dark blue suit that she'd never seen before. Every hair was in place, and his eyes held a good-humored sparkle that set the hairs on the back of her neck quivering in alarm.

It was simply not fair, Kit thought. There ought to be a law. No man should be allowed to be so good-looking and so incredibly sensual at that hour of the morning.

He looked around the tiny living room. "Cozy place."

"You can say that again. But then I'm seldom here except to sleep, so it doesn't matter much." She took her coat from the hall closet.

Almost absentmindedly, he held it for her. Even after Kit had slid her arms into the sleeves, however, he continued to hold the lapels. His hands lay lightly across her shoulders. When Kit turned her head in puzzlement to see what had absorbed his attention, her dangling earring brushed his wrist. The contact set off an electrical tingle that raced through every nerve in Kit's body.

You are a sad case, Deevers, she told herself.

Kit couldn't seem to force herself to step away. It wasn't as if he was holding her. The weight of his hands was barely noticeable. But other things seemed to form a web that was more effective. His cologne was little more than a breath of scent, but it seemed to paralyze her. His warmth made her want to nestle against his body and close her eyes and relax....

There was a reason, Kit thought irritably, that executions by firing squad were always held at dawn. It was the hour when the human body was least able to put up a fight!

"If we're going to make it in time for the show, we'd better get going," she said.

"What? Oh, I'm sorry—I was just admiring your taste in furniture."

"Courtesy of an aunt who owned an antique shop."

"Do you mean the furniture or the taste?"

"Both, actually. She taught me to trust my instincts about what I like, and then she bought it for me wholesale."

"Nice person to know."

The air was still night-crisp, though the eastern sky was beginning to glow. As they walked toward the Porsche, Kit saw the first streetlight wink out as dawn approached.

Jarrett said abruptly, "I've been thinking, Kitten."

"So early in the morning? That could be dangerous."

"What have you planned for after the auction?"

"A champagne toast to celebrate my survival. Why? What have you got in mind?"

"It occurred to me that after all the excitement and hype, just saying thanks and sending everyone home might be a bit anticlimactic—especially for the women who bought the dream dates."

Kit frowned. "Now that you mention it... So what do you suggest we do instead?"

"We turn up the lights and have a party. It would be a chance for the buyers to meet their dates and for the women who didn't succeed in buying a package to wind down and have a good time anyway."

"Great," Kit said crisply. "You're in charge. And before you start fussing about the responsibility, remember that I only agreed to raise the money—and by the time the party starts, I'll have kept my part of the bargain.''

"Was I fussing? The party *was* my idea, after all."

His tone was so mild, so cooperative, that every nerve cell in Kit's body began to shriek warnings. But she could hardly withdraw permission now. And no matter what he planned, a party after the auction surely couldn't hurt the outcome where fund-raising was concerned. Could it?

Dawn was streaking the sky as they passed the security guard at the back door of the television station. They were ushered into the green room to wait for their segment to begin. Jarrett got them each a cup of poisonous-looking coffee from a machine in the corner, but before Kit could try a sip, a young aide came to take them onto the set, and she gratefully set the cup aside.

The background was painted a vibrant blue, which made Kit's eyes hurt almost as much as did the bright lights. She could hardly concentrate on the host as he introduced himself, and there was barely time for a deep breath before the commercial break came to a close.

"There's nothing to be nervous about," Jarrett said under his breath.

If you knew what I have in mind, Kit thought, *you wouldn't be so certain of that.*

The host began to talk about the auction and turned to Jarrett with his first question.

Kit tipped her head and looked at Jarrett with the shy, worshipful glow she'd practiced in her bathroom mirror for an hour last night. She only hoped she didn't look as silly as she felt.

Jarrett didn't seem to notice. "But those details are really Kit's part of the event," he finished, and flashed a smile at her.

The host turned to Kit. "There's been some discussion in the press of disagreement between the two of you about the auction," he said.

He couldn't have given her a better opening if she'd scripted it herself. Kit braced herself—it was now or never. "Oh, no. In fact..." She flashed the shy-but-proud smile of a woman who's just gained her greatest desire and said, "Of course there's nothing *official* till after the auction, but Jarrett and I..." She paused and did her best to look adorably confused. "But I shouldn't have mentioned that here, should I, darling? About the engagement?"

Jarrett drew a sharp breath. Kit thought it quite likely, considering the sensitive microphone he was wearing, that viewers all over Chicago heard it just as clearly as she did. She wanted to cheer.

"You little *wretch*," he said under his breath.

Kit clapped both hands over her mouth. She'd anticipated that he would be caught off guard, but she'd never dreamed he would react so strongly. She only hoped the laugh she was trying so hard to stifle would look like badly handled hysteria.

Jarrett seized her wrists and pulled her hands away from her face. "All I can say is—" His other arm slid around her shoulders with the taut strength of a steel cable.

He had pulled her slightly off balance, so she was leaning into him, and with his left hand still holding both her wrists, there was no way for Kit to get enough leverage to free herself.

All right, a little voice at the back of her brain whispered. *How are you going to maneuver yourself out of this one, Deevers?*

Then Jarrett's mouth came down firmly on hers, and Kit forgot all about struggling. The kiss she had imagined in her office yesterday had been powerful enough to light up Chicago, but the reality was enough to blow every electrical grid in the country.

Kit's heart seemed to shudder to a halt. Time itself slowed till cold molasses would have seemed speedy in comparison.

Not that Kit cared. Her world had narrowed until it held only the taste of him, the scent of him, the feel of him. And when eventually he stopped kissing her, Kit's eyes wouldn't focus, and breathing was nothing more than a dim memory. If it hadn't been for his arm still tight around her, she'd probably have slid off her chair.

Jarrett released her wrists and gently shook a fingertip in her face. "Keeping me in suspense like this and then giving me my answer on television." He turned to the host and added calmly, "Don't you think she's a wretch to do that?"

The host was opening and closing his mouth like a fish gasping for oxygen.

Kit hadn't realized how hot it was on the set. She was burning up. She wanted to fan herself, but the muscles in her arms didn't seem to work anymore.

"Well, ladies and gentlemen, you heard it here first," the host said finally. "I suppose this means you won't be offering a package after all, Jarrett? I mean, since you're pretty much taken now—"

Jarrett smiled at Kit, still leaning helplessly against his shoulder. "Oh, I've certainly been *taken*," he murmured.

With the speed and clarity of the visions experienced by drowning swimmers, Kit suddenly saw the Dream Dates Auction going down the drain. All her planning, her work and her effort were in vain, because she'd miscalculated so badly when she'd planned this prank. And she'd handed Jarrett the perfect opportunity not only to get out of the auction, but to make her look like an incompetent fool in the bargain.

Which was exactly what he'd wanted from the beginning.

"Oh, not at all," he said cheerfully. "Kit's a wonderful, understanding, terrific woman, and she's in full support of this excellent cause. That's why she said that we won't make anything absolutely official till afterward."

"Oh." The host, obviously at sea, looked toward the control room as if he wanted to beg for help. "Well, thank you two for—"

Jarrett went on relentlessly. "Naturally, this confirms my suspicion that she's been planning all along to bid for me. And I'm sure it'll be safe for everyone else at the auction to offer any amount of money, since—under the circumstances—my Kitten obviously plans to top all other bids. I'm right, aren't I, Kit?"

"Umm—" Kit said.

Jarrett looked at her lovingly. He did it, Kit thought irritably, with tremendous skill—far more than she'd displayed when she'd tried earlier to put across her shy and worshipful gaze.

"But of course you will," Jarrett went on smoothly. "Because you wouldn't want to let any other woman go with me on our honeymoon—would you, darling?"

They were hardly outside the station before Jarrett leaned against the cinder-block wall of the building and burst into raucous laughter. "The look on your face, Kitten—"

Kit tapped her toe on the pavement. "Dammit, Jarrett, that was not fair!"

"Oh? And what you did *was*, I suppose?"

She bit her lip.

"That's what I thought. Come on, darling, let's declare ourselves even. One thing about it, you won't have any trouble filling that ballroom now.''

He was right about that much. ''Exactly,'' Kit said. ''Wasn't it clever of me to think of that stunt? And of course, I'm so pleased that you had the wit to play along.''

''Right,'' Jarrett said dryly. ''I'm sure you had it planned out in advance, down to the last detail. Tell me, darling—was that the sort of kiss you had in mind, or do you want to show me a more effective style?''

The very idea of kissing him again made Kit's insides feel like melted marshmallows. ''It was good enough to get by.''

He swept her a bow. ''Halfhearted praise from you, my dear, is better than a gold medal from the ordinary woman.''

Kit almost added that no amount of practice would do him any good, but just in time she thought better of the jab. Such a feeble thrust wasn't likely to pierce Jarrett's self-confidence. Besides, she realized that what she'd intended as insult was probably true—obviously he *didn't* have much left to learn about the art of the kiss.

Outside Tryad's brownstone, Jarrett parked the Porsche by the fireplug, helped Kit out and said goodbye.

She was relieved that he wasn't going to be sitting beside her desk all day, but she couldn't help taking one more jab at him. ''Leaving so soon? I thought you were going to devote the rest of this week to the auction, and there's still four full business days left.''

''I just have to run an errand or two, but I'll be back. And then I'll be working very hard, indeed.'' His voice was a soft drawl. ''After all, I still have to plan—how shall I say it?—the honeymoon you deserve.''

*   *   *

An hour later Kit was still shuffling papers and trying to concentrate when she heard the front door slam and the distinctive sound of Susannah's step on the stairway.

Susannah didn't even take off her coat or set her brief-case down before she came into Kit's office. "And you call *me* the creative one!" she announced.

"I take it you saw the television show?"

"At my wildest, I'd never have pulled anything that crazy."

"It's a defective gene," Kit muttered. She was half serious. She must possess some self-destructive instinct, some flaw that not only made her continually challenge Jarrett, but worse, led her to believe there was a chance she might someday come out ahead.

"So what was it like to kiss him?" Susannah tossed herself down on the chaise.

The jealousy Kit had felt earlier in the week echoed faintly through her mind. Was there something more than idle curiosity about Susannah's question? Jarrett had announced that he liked Susannah. Did that work both ways?

"You don't want to know," Alison announced from the doorway.

"What do you mean, Ali? Of course, I want to know."

"Well, Kit doesn't want to tell you. Here." Alison set a tall glass of water and an aspirin bottle on Kit's desk blotter. "I thought you might need a little some-thing after the show this morning."

Kit said, gratefully, "You're a jewel, Ali." She swal-lowed two tablets. "I've got it. I'll just resign and check myself into an asylum—"

"Aspirin and a padded cell?" Susannah shook her head. "I'd have thought he'd be better at kissing than *that*."

"Before the auction's finished?" Alison sounded horrified. "Don't think you're going to get by with passing the buck to us."

Kit went on. "You two can have a news conference to announce you're seeking a new partner, and then it won't matter what Jarrett does to try to ruin the auction."

"Why would he want to?" Alison said briskly. "I never have understood that, you know."

"Because—" Kit paused. She'd come this far on her own, keeping Jarrett's threat against Tryad to herself. Why worry her partners now, when the auction was looking like a success despite her foolish behavior? Jarrett had admitted that after this morning's performance, the tickets should sell themselves.

And Alison was right—why would he go to so much trouble if he was planning to sabotage the event?

Not so much trouble after all, Kit reminded herself darkly. He'd suggested the players on his basketball team as prizes but refused to ask them to participate. He arranged for hors d'oeuvres, but that hadn't been helping so much as getting himself out of having to work. What had Jarrett really *done,* besides take up space in Kit's office, distract her from work at all hours of the day and blow bubbles?

Maybe, she thought, she owed Susannah and Alison a warning. The trouble was that once uttered, the words could never be unsaid. Perhaps it would be best to wait a little while, at least till her head didn't hurt and she could think more logically, to decide.

"Maybe he doesn't," Kit said. "Maybe it's just me he wants to ruin."

Susannah's grin was wicked. "In the best tradition of a Victorian novel, no doubt." She moved off the chaise and went to stand by the window. "You could let down

your hair from this window like Rapunzel, I suppose—
Hey, look at this!''

"His sister's a victim," Alison said.

Kit was stunned. "What?''

Susannah said, "I mean it, guys, you've got to see
this. Mrs. Holcomb's shooing the paparazzo out from
under the bushes!"

Alison rushed for the window. Kit, feeling the weight
of responsibility, headed for the stairs instead.

She threw open the front door just as the recluse next
door—the woman none of them had ever seen leave her
house before—bent over the juniper bushes, broom in
hand.

Heedless of her high-heeled pumps, Kit took the steps
from porch to sidewalk in a single leap. The jolt to her
ankles slowed her down, and before she could reach the
street, Jarrett's Porsche pulled into a parking space a few
feet from the fireplug.

A legal parking spot, Kit thought. Now that was a
novelty, for Jarrett.

He stepped out and leaned against his open door. "I'm
delighted you're so anxious to see me that you've come
rushing out here, darling, but—'' He followed Kit's gaze
to the scene across the street.

Kit winced as she heard the broomstick striking the
photographer's shoulders, followed by a voice as shrill
as a squeaking hinge. "You think women are helpless,
do you? Well, this'll teach you not to spy!''

Jarrett crossed the street in three steps, removed the
broom from Mrs. Holcomb's grip and briskly shook her
hand. "I see you've caught a window peeker, ma'am.
Good work, you deserve a commendation. I'll take care
of this now. Thank you very much for your help.''

Mrs. Holcomb grumbled for a moment, then—as if
she'd abruptly realized where she was—she seized her

broom and scuttled toward her front door like a cockroach frightened of the light.

The photographer put both hands up, palms out, and backed off. "Crazy old lady was trying to kill me," he said defensively. "I was only doing my job!"

"Yes, yes," Jarrett said. "But maybe you'd better keep your distance anyway. I see you're wearing a pager. Give me the number and I'll keep you posted about where we'll be. You won't have to get scratched up by the junipers to get your pictures, the recluse can celebrate driving you away, and everybody will be happy."

The photographer made a feeble effort to smooth out his clothes. "Yeah, sure you will," he said, but he handed over a card and retreated down the block.

Kit hadn't said a word.

With the field cleared of combatants, Jarrett dusted off his hands and smiled at her.

Deep inside Kit, a spark that she'd tried for days to deny grew slowly into the steady flame of knowledge.

He took her arm. "How do you feel about two weeks on the south coast of France?"

The flame roared higher until it threatened to consume her, and she had to face the truth she had tried so hard to ignore.

She wasn't just attracted to Jarrett. She wasn't simply captivated by his charm. She didn't merely find him physically seductive. No, the truth was much worse than any of those.

Somewhere in the last few days, she'd looked past the playboy to the man, and she'd fallen in love with him.

It wasn't just attraction she felt. She couldn't shake him off as she'd joked she would, like a troublesome head cold. This case of love was a whole lot more serious than that.

CHAPTER NINE

As SHE STOOD THERE, the fires of truth burned away delusion and left Kit facing the stark skeleton of fact. She'd thought she was immune to him, but she'd been hiding from her feelings since the beginning. From the instant they'd met, she'd felt the tug of attraction, as if something deep inside her knew that this was the man of her destiny.

When she'd so unexpectedly—and literally—run into him at the reception following the fashion show, he'd caught her. But she'd thought her breathless, weightless feeling as he'd held her upright had been only shock at encountering him once more.

Then there was his offer to help with the auction—or what she'd believed at the time was an offer to help— by recruiting the basketball players to take part. She'd experienced a burst of joy and told herself it was because the success of the auction was assured and Tryad was safe. But neither of those things, really, had been the source of her delight. It had been the idea of Jarrett helping, of him believing in her—and the image of them working together.

What a mess, Kit told herself. *You've really gotten yourself into a spot this time, Deevers.*

The worst thing of all, though, was knowing that Jarrett's joke about a honeymoon was no longer a joke to her. There was nothing she would like more than to be his wife, his love, forever.

And there was nothing farther from her reach.

"Kitten? Does it take you that long to decide, or are

we playing twenty questions while I guess where you'd like to go instead? What *would* be your idea of the perfect honeymoon?''

Anything that includes you. But she'd be a fool even to think about that, for fear the fact would show in her eyes. If he was to guess and he laughed at her...

He hadn't really been asking her, anyway, she realized. Not about France, not about the perfect honeymoon. He'd been speculating, as if to himself. The question had been entirely rhetorical.

''The south coast of France,'' Kit said slowly, as if debating. ''You mean the Riviera? Casinos and nightlife and glitz and glamour? Some of the women coming Saturday night might like that.'' She shook her head. ''But it's not my cup of tea.''

''Of course I don't mean the Riviera. I thought we'd sleep under a cardboard box on the sand and beachcomb for items of value to trade for food.''

''Of course—I should have known the ordinary wouldn't appeal to you.'' Deliberately, she kept her voice tart. ''But wouldn't you rather have six months in an army tent in Iceland?''

''Oh, certainly, if that's what you'd like. I'll have to add fur trim to your black lace outfit, though.''

''I thought you'd decided on the white. But never mind. I wouldn't want you to ruin the lines of a Webster design.''

''It would be a problem to make it look as if it belonged,'' Jarrett agreed. ''If you want adventure, though, there's always a camel trek across the Sahara Desert. At least it would be warm.''

''No, thanks. Blowing sand would be too harsh on my skin.''

''That's true. And when you're wearing only lace,

there's a lot of skin to be harsh to.'' He paused on the porch.

"Are you coming in?'' She dared a glance at him.

"No, I was just passing by and thought I'd try out my idea.''

"Well, don't rack your brain too hard. I'm afraid we're not going to be able to work this out.''

"You're surely not giving up already? How high are you prepared to bid, anyway?''

"I'll check the contents of my piggy bank this afternoon and let you know.'' She shut the door of Tryad's brownstone in his face and went upstairs.

Susannah was in her office next to Kit's, her head bent over a folder open on her desk. Her pose was a bit too sanctimonious to be real, Kit thought. She paused in the doorway. "I'm glad to see you're working instead of hanging out the window watching.''

Susannah looked up with a sunny smile. "Would I do anything like that?''

"Of course you would.''

"Well, all right, I did. But not after you got onto the porch, where the roof blocked my view.''

"That's what I thought.''

"Someone had to make sure you were safe.''

"From Mrs. Holcomb? She's harmless.''

"I don't think the paparazzo would agree with you. Besides, that wasn't what I meant. I thought for a minute that the knight in shining armor was going to turn you over his knee.''

"Better that than—'' Kit saw the bright interest in Susannah's eyes and broke off abruptly. "I'd better get to work. There's just three full days left till the auction.''

"Save me a ticket,'' Susannah called after her. "I'm not about to miss this show!''

*   *   *

Jarrett didn't come back to the office, but he started calling every few hours with another suggestion for a honeymoon destination. Some were outrageous, others almost reasonable—and Kit wasn't sure which agitated her more. The off-the-wall ideas were a painful reminder that Jarrett was nowhere near as serious about her as she was about him. The inviting ones only made her heart ache worse as she pictured the way things might have been.

The truth was, she wouldn't care whether the destination was luxurious or silly or humble. If he loved her, she'd go anywhere with him—the South Seas or the South of France, a box on a sunny beach or a tent on the Icelandic shore...or nowhere at all. If he loved her the way she loved him, nothing would matter as long as she could be with him.

But each call reminded her that to him, this was nothing more than a grand jest—a practical joke she'd brought on herself by embarrassing him on television. And she was doing nothing but asking for trouble if she allowed herself to pretend it was anything else.

So instead of telling him not to call, or instructing Rita not to put him through, she listened to each incredible plan and laughed and commended him and suggested that he try a little harder.

And each time, her heartache grew, for the Dream Dates Auction was growing closer, and she knew that one of these suggestions would become reality. The long weekend in Hawaii, perhaps, or the golfing trip to Palm Springs, or the theater tour of London would be listed on the program and offered up for sale. On Saturday night some lucky woman would be the winning bidder, and not long after, she would go off on a trip with Jarrett.

The trip that should have been Kit's.

He'd been dead on target with his parting shot at the

television station. The last thing she wanted to do was let him go off on a honeymoon trip—even one that wasn't really a honeymoon—without her.

But there was nothing she could do about it.

She even, in a moment of craziness, added up all her financial resources and contemplated blowing every penny at the auction. But though the sum was respectable, it was likely to be no competition for the sort of women who were buying tickets in droves.

And in any case, she knew the money didn't really make any difference. If she had all the cash in the world, she wouldn't bid on him—because winning him in name only would simply be pretending. And pretending would lead nowhere but to pain.

Better to leave the whole thing behind her. She would get through the auction, and smile at the winning bidder, and congratulate her, and wish them a happy trip. She might even send a bon-voyage bouquet.

And she would never let Jarrett guess that it was a goodbye gift, as well.

Their television appearance had created a momentum that threatened to sweep Kit off her feet. As the last days before the auction ticked away, the fever grew. Every few hours another vendor phoned, out of tickets and pleading for more. There seemed to be a permanent lineup of bachelors on hold, waiting for Kit to get around to them. When *USA Today* called to ask for press credentials, Kit put down the telephone and screamed in delight.

Of course, there was a downside, too. Rita was threatening to quit her job—if only, she said, the telephone would stop ringing long enough to let her reach the door. By the end of the week, Kit was half-expecting the secretary to rip all the phone wires from the wall, drape them around her neck and go screaming like a banshee down the street.

Susannah quietly took over all Kit's regular work. Kit was too busy to wonder why her clients suddenly seemed to have gone underground, until she overheard Susannah explaining airily to one of Kit's clients that he hadn't been able to get through to Kit because—unfortunately for him—he wasn't a bachelor.

Alison made sure they all ate on a regular and healthy basis. Not only did she put food in front of Kit, but she waited patiently until it was consumed before she'd go away.

Even the calico cat who lived in the production room looked a little dazed by the sudden clamor of her surroundings. She took to sleeping in the farthest, darkest corner of the storage closet on the lower level, next to Alison's office. When Rita got a new box of telephone message slips from the closet one day and shut the door tight, even the cat didn't notice for several hours.

Kit added *Make amends to cat* to her list of things to do as soon as the auction was over. At least, she told herself, she could manage that—a catnip mouse and a good session of petting should do the trick. She was afraid she'd never be able to make it up to Alison, Susannah and Rita.

On Friday afternoon she left a terse message for Jarrett that if he expected his dream date to be included in the program he'd better call her before the day was out.

A couple of hours later, he appeared in her office, pulled up a chair beside her desk and waited patiently until she was off the telephone. "Did you know all your lines are jammed?" he asked politely. "I tried to call. In fact, I've been trying to call all day. I've had such a lot of good ideas—"

The tone of his voice was enough to create pictures

in Kit's mind. An igloo and a white bearskin rug…the fountain gardens of a castle in Spain…

It was just as well, she told herself, that the phone lines had been jammed. She could manufacture enough scenarios by herself, without any help at all from him, to keep her mind spinning.

"Well, prune them down to one," she ordered, "and stick to it, all right? I've got about two more hours to finish the program, and if you don't decide this minute, I'll put up a chalkboard outside the ballroom tomorrow and write you in as the special of the day."

"Bachelor de jour, you mean?" Jarrett frowned. "But it depends."

"On what? If you haven't decided by now—"

"For one thing, you still haven't told me how much you're willing to pay for me."

Kit swiveled her chair to face him. "That's because I didn't want to hurt your feelings when I realized my piggy bank contains only fourteen dollars and seventy-three cents. And it's mostly in pennies, to boot."

He nodded wisely. "Is that why tickets are so scarce? You held them back so there'd be less competition for your bid?"

"As a matter of fact, they're almost sold out." Kit knew she sounded proud of herself, and she saw no reason she shouldn't be. With ticket sales alone—less the expenses of the ballroom rental, the special help she'd had to hire to run the event and the printing costs, of course—she was well on the way to carrying out her promise.

"Of course it remains to be seen whether everyone comes," he said thoughtfully. "And, having come, if they bid."

"You just can't admit that I might pull this off, can

you? Tomorrow, after it's all over, I'll be happy to accept your apology. In the meantime—"

"Two weeks on my private Caribbean island. And that's my final offer."

"You *own* a Caribbean island?"

"Only a small one." His tone was dismissive. "No resorts, no cruise ships, no nightlife. Just a lot of white sand and a very small bungalow. It's called Paradise."

It *sounded* like paradise to Kit. A paradise, of course, that she would never see. She had to swallow hard before she could say, "Do you want to write up the sales pitch, or shall I?"

"Be my guest," Jarrett offered.

She only wished she could—but there would be plenty of time for daydreaming and regrets after this was all over.

Kit reached for a pen. "What's included? Snorkeling? Fishing? Sailing?"

Jarrett nodded. "Lying lazily on a beach towel. Sipping champagne on the terrace. Swimming in the moonlight. Whatever you—I mean, whatever the winner wants."

Kit crafted a couple of sentences and tossed the notebook to him.

Jarrett read it and tossed it back. "Sounds like more than fourteen dollars' worth to me."

"I guess you'll have the adventure of a new woman in your life, then." She tore the page out of the notebook and slipped it in the folder of program materials, ready to take to the printer. "The etiquette people wouldn't approve if I bought you, anyway."

"Why not?"

Kit smiled, though it took all her self-control. "Because all the books agree—a woman can't pay for her own honeymoon. And I'm sure, when it's something so important, you wouldn't want it to look improper. Would you?''

With the list of dream dates safely in the hands of the printer and a faithful promise that two thousand copies would be waiting for her late tomorrow afternoon in the Englin Hotel's grand ballroom, Kit finally had time to take a deep breath.

She was surprised to find, when she stepped onto the street from the printers' storefront shop, that the air felt almost warm. While she'd been buried in her office with every thought focused on the auction, spring had crept up on Chicago. In a winter-ravaged flower bed just outside the print shop, tiny crocus leaves poked through sand left over from the winter's snow removal. Across the street was a florist, and on impulse Kit went in and bought a sheaf of creamy white tulips and brilliant yellow jonquils and something else, a pinkish-purple bloom that she didn't recognize.

With the flowers cradled in her arms, she walked slowly to Tryad. There were still plenty of things to be done, though it was mostly a matter of checking and rechecking and tying up loose ends.

Susannah was coming out of the office with a portfolio under her arm just as Kit came up the street. She eyed the flowers. ''If you're practicing the wedding march, Kitty, I think you're holding that bouquet at the wrong angle.''

''As a matter of fact,'' Kit began. The corner of the lace curtain next door fluttered, and Kit waved, almost in relief, when she realized it was the first time since the paparazzo incident that she'd seen any sign of normal life from the recluse. ''Actually, they're for Mrs. Holcomb,'' she said. ''Sort of a thank-you for routing the paparazzo.''

"She'll never answer the door," Susannah warned. "Much less let you in."

Kit climbed the steps to the front porch, which should have been a twin to Tryad's. The paint was peeling, however, and the mailbox looked as if it had served only as a home for spiders for the last five years.

She rang the bell and heard a shuffling inside. Finally, with a creak that sounded like a mausoleum vault, the door opened a slit. All Kit could see through the crack was a single watery blue eye under a bushy gray brow.

At least I got through Susannah's first obstacle, Kit thought. "I'm from the office next door," she began.

"Yes?" The voice was curt. "What d'you want?"

"I brought you some flowers." Kit held up the cellophane-wrapped sheaf.

"Don't need any," Mrs. Holcomb announced.

Nice conversation stopper, Kit thought. *Now what do I do?*

"I thought you might like them anyway," she said. "It's sort of a peace offering for the fuss in the neighborhood lately, and a thank-you for defending us all from that photographer."

The silence stretched out painfully.

"I'll leave them out here," Kit said finally, and stooped to lay the flowers on the threshold.

"You mean—they're free?" The old woman's voice cracked.

Kit's heart twisted. "They're a present, yes."

Slowly, with a creak that sounded painful, the door opened wider.

"Tulips," Mrs. Holcomb said. Her fingertip trembled as she stroked the flower petals. "And jonquils. And larkspur."

Kit put the sheaf in the woman's arms. "Is that what those are? I wasn't sure."

"Always liked tulips better than roses. Flashy flowers, roses."

"They are, aren't they?"

There was a gleam of tears in the old woman's eyes. "I never was the flashy sort."

"Neither am I," Kit said dryly. "But there's nothing wrong with good and solid."

Afraid to press her luck, she said goodbye and walked to Tryad.

Rita had gone home, and Alison was standing at the copy machine in the front office. "I haven't seen you moving this slowly in a couple of weeks, Kitty," she said. "I shouldn't think the letdown would hit till Sunday, at least, the way you've been going."

"The worst is over, I think. And I just realized even Mrs. Holcomb has hidden depths."

Alison paused in the midst of collating a copy. "Now that sounds like a philosophical lecture I'd like to hear."

"It could be, I suppose, but I'm too tired to think about it." Kit perched on the corner of Rita's desk. "We were interrupted the other day just as you were telling me about Jarrett's sister."

Alison shrugged. "I don't know much. I read it somewhere, but I can't even remember where, now." She smiled. "It was before he loomed large in our lives, you see, so I had no idea it would be important."

"What do you remember?"

"Just that he had a sister whose husband beat her while they were married and stalked her after she finally divorced him. She lives in Europe, I think the article said, and she's very careful about her travels and activities even yet, because of her ex."

"I don't blame her. I'd run, too. But at least that explains why Jarrett doesn't talk about her." Kit could understand, now that she knew how close he had been

to the effects of violence, why he'd taken the failure of
the fashion show so personally. If it had been a cause
he felt less strongly about, the botched show might not
have mattered as much. But it did. The spectacular flop
had left his favorite charity dangling. And from his
standpoint—with Colette and Heather as witnesses—the
failure had looked like Kit's fault from start to finish.

Kit could understand why he'd been furious, why he'd
insisted that she make up for the mess he thought she'd
caused, even why he'd threatened Tryad. She could
make allowances for Jarrett's being quick to judge the
whole firm. The firm was fairly new and small, and in
an effort to become better known, they'd taken on an
awfully lot of charity business. For all he knew, they
were a fly-by-night operation out to line their own pock-
ets at the expense of a good cause.

But come Saturday night, he was going to know better. Kit would prove herself with flying colors.

She had a right to be pleased. She was not only dem-
onstrating her worth as a public relations person, but
she'd done it on her own—with the help of her partners,
of course, but none to speak of from Jarrett. It was certainly no thanks to him that she'd have a complete list
of dream dates on Saturday night.

She'd done it by herself, and he simply had to be
delighted with the results. A good cause would receive
a very large donation, Tryad would get all kinds of good
publicity, and Jarrett would be so happy...

So happy that he'll see you in a completely new light.

That, Kit told herself tartly, was a fairy tale. And she
knew better than to dream of Prince Charming.

The ballroom was awash in activity when Kit arrived,
wearing jeans and with a garment bag draped over her
shoulder, two hours before the auction was to start.

There was no point in coming earlier, Carl the concierge had told her, because the ballroom had been booked for midday, and the only thing she could do was stand around till that event was over.

But obviously things had run later than he'd expected. Workers had just started stripping tables of used linen when she came in, and Kit, horrified, closed her eyes and counted to fifty in a feeble effort to calm herself.

They do this all the time, she told herself. *They'll be ready.*

Carl, in the midst of directing the legions of waiters, spotted her and called, "There's a bunch of boxes for you. I had them dumped out on the mezzanine, since the crowd was still in here."

"Great." Kit laid her garment bag over the back of a chair and went in search of the boxes. *At least the programs are present and accounted for. Now if the people just come...*

She hadn't stopped to think how large a space two thousand programs would take. There were ten large boxes stacked on the mezzanine floor. She looked around for a bellman to haul them to the ballroom, but soon gave up. It appeared that every spare hand was already at work inside.

She tore the tape off the first box and took out a program. It looked perfect—elegant and professional—and the list of dream dates was impressive.

Not a bad show for less than three weeks' work. Kit congratulated herself. Jarrett would certainly be pleased. Maybe he'd even be proud.

Back to that again, are we, Deevers? Don't count on it.

Carl came in search of her. "This buffet line," he began. "I forgot to ask if you need steam tables or just space for cold things."

So much for Kit's moment of self-satisfaction. She hadn't even thought of that problem. "I don't know," she said unhappily. "I'm sorry, Carl—but I'm not sure what we're getting in the way of snacks."

He rolled his eyes. "That's what happens when you take your chances on donations, Kit. I'll set them both up, just in case."

One by one, she carried the boxes of programs to the ballroom door and stacked them next to the ticket booth. Inside, the transformation was under way. At one side of the ballroom the afternoon's head table was becoming a stage. The round banquet tables had been pulled into a new pattern, leaving an open space in the center of the room to create a better view for each seat, and most of the tables were draped in spotless white linen.

Her ticket takers and ushers, hired for the occasion, started to drift in for their instructions. By the time she got them all in place, less than an hour remained. She'd have just enough time to change her clothes and greet the bachelors before the evening swung into high gear.

Kit retrieved her garment bag and hurried down the length of the almost deserted mezzanine toward the nearest ladies' room. Her dress, borrowed at the last possible instant from Susannah's closet, was dark blue silk, with long sleeves and absolutely no back. Not that she was trying to impress anyone, least of all Jarrett—but if her shoulder blades really were her best feature, Kit had decided she might as well make the best of them.

By the time she was dressed, ticket holders were starting to gather on the mezzanine outside the ballroom, but there were still no hors d'oeuvres in sight. Kit felt the first flutters of panic in her midsection and stormed through the ballroom on her way backstage, looking for Jarrett.

In the small room set aside for them, Chicago's most

eligible bachelors had gathered. Some were charmingly nervous as they awaited their turn on the auction block. Others were completely cool, as if they did this every day.

And one—the very one she was seeking, of course—was nowhere to be seen.

Kit told herself that without a doubt Jarrett would stroll in at the last instant, happy to have kept her on edge as long as possible. But he wouldn't dare stand her up completely. Would he?

There were, of course, the missing hors d'oeuvres. Or had they ever existed? Had he sabotaged her, after all?

If he had, she thought grimly, she'd rewrite his offer and auction him off to the *lowest* bidder.

She handed a program to every bachelor and climbed atop a chair to draw their attention. "I want to thank you all for taking part in raising money for such an important cause," she began. "I can't begin to tell you how much your contribution is appreciated, and I hope that you'll all have barrels of fun in carrying out your—"

Jarrett appeared in the doorway, looking calm and unruffled, and Kit's sudden relief almost derailed her train of thought.

"Your dream date," she went on. "The program lists you alphabetically, since it seemed the only fair way, and that's the order in which we'll auction the packages. If there are any questions..."

There didn't seem to be. Kit scrambled from her unsteady perch and headed for the door, but by the time she got there Jarrett had vanished once more. One of the bachelors pointed toward the hallway. "If you're looking for Webster, he went out there."

The hallway was lined with banquet equipment, and she had to dodge a couple of maintenance men who were moving excess tables from the ballroom. But a few feet down the hall was Jarrett, leaning against the wall, hands behind his back. His tux was immaculate, his bow tie perfect, every hair in place.

Facing him was Heather, in a silver-sequined gown far too sophisticated for her. "Mother said she might let me bid," the girl was saying, "so some hussy can't buy you."

That, Kit thought, was almost a contradiction in terms.

Jarrett turned his head and smiled at Kit, a slow, warm smile that acted like adrenaline on the butterflies in her stomach. "And I didn't even *ask* her," he murmured. "I don't suppose there was any particular hussy she wanted to protect me from?"

"I hate to interrupt something so important as an attempt to fix the auction," Kit said, "but there's a little matter of some hors d'oeuvres you promised, Jarrett."

From behind his back he produced a small white waxed-paper bag. Kit took it warily and unfolded the top. The mouth-watering scent of a bacon-wrapped mushroom floated out to greet her. Under it she could see a pizza a little larger than a thumbnail and something that looked like a miniature broccoli quiche. "Lovely," she said crisply. "But if this is what you call snacks for two thousand, you'd better get out your pocket knife and start slicing."

"There are about half a billion more out in the ballroom. I just didn't think it would look good for you to push to the head of the line to get a taste, so I brought you samples of the best stuff."

The butterflies settled down a bit. She should have trusted him, Kit thought. He might not have provided much help with this event—aside, perhaps, from the hors d'oeuvres—but she couldn't recite a specific example of him working *against* her, either. Unless she counted camping in her office and distracting her...

He'd turned to Heather. "So Colette sent you here to reassure me?" He reached out to ruffle her hair.

Heather stepped quickly aside. "No. I just thought you should know, so you wouldn't worry."

"Tell her thanks, but there's no need for her to get involved. And as for you, Heather, you can't bid because you're not an adult. Run along, now, all right?"

"Well, I'm certainly no child." Heather sniffed, but she did as Jarrett asked.

Kit was still holding the bacon-wrapped mushroom. "You mean you don't want to spend two weeks in the Caribbean with Heather and Colette?"

"It wouldn't be the first time," he said. "It's become a Webster family retreat. Do you like the snacks?"

Reflexively, she lifted the mushroom almost to her mouth. "They're family?" she asked before she could think better of it.

Was Heather's mother Jarrett's elusive sister? The idea made sense, for abuse could account for the hard edges Colette and Heather displayed. Perhaps the story of living in Europe was only a cover-up to keep the troublesome ex-husband from looking too hard. And this explained the way Jarrett had talked to Heather at Milady Lingerie and again tonight. He'd sounded almost like an exasperated uncle, and maybe that was exactly what he was.

The corner of his mouth curved. "What's that mean?" His voice was soft, suggestive. "Kitten, surely you're not jealous!"

Kit knew she sounded defensive. "I was just making conversation. It had nothing to do with—"

"Oh, I don't agree. You're not the sort to waste time with trivial things, Kitten." His hand slipped to the back of her neck and pulled her close. "I think it means...this."

His kiss was everything she'd ever dreamed it could be, and more—soft and tantalizing one instant, firm and almost demanding the next. By turns he was caressing, tormenting, playful, gentle, seductive, but always unpredictable. The only things Kit knew were that she could not bear to have it end—and that it must.

But not immediately. Surely there was no sin in enjoying this instant, this last opportunity to pretend for a moment that he was really hers....

She thought the buzz in her brain was oxygen deprivation—the inevitable result of forgetting how to breathe—until Jarrett raised his head and frowned. "I think the crowd in the ballroom's getting restless," he said. "Want me to go round up the sacrificial lambs?"

She couldn't answer. Her throat was too tight with impossible dreams, with unshed tears, with words she could never say.

He raised her hand to his lips, frowned and unfolded her fingers from around a very misshapen bacon-wrapped mushroom. He nipped it from her palm with a sensual brush of his tongue and licked away the juices it had left behind. By the time he let go of her hand and turned toward the backstage room to fetch the bachelors, Kit felt as if her whole body had turned to gelatin.

The lights in the ballroom were turned low, and the spotlights focused on the stage were almost blinding. As Kit led the procession, the crowd's rustle and banter dropped almost to silence and then swelled into applause.

But nothing—not the noise, the lights or even the singsong voice of the auctioneer—seemed real to Kit. She could see only Jarrett's face, feel the strength of his arms around her, smell bacon and mushroom mixed with his cologne. She went through the motions without pause, without error—ushering each bachelor from his seat in the semicircle to stand beside the auctioneer and then, when the hammer fell on the final bid, showing him to the stairs at one end of the stage so he could take his seat in the reserved section of the ballroom.

Eventually, she got used to the lights. She could not only move around the stage without wanting to shield her eyes, but she could see into the audience, pick out faces and watch the bidding proceed. They were almost to the end.

"Jarrett Webster," the auctioneer's voice boomed, and automatically Kit turned to the side of the stage. He rose to meet her, took both her hands and whispered, "You *are* going to bid, of course?"

"All fourteen dollars' worth," she answered, and left him beside the auctioneer's podium.

She felt as if she'd torn out her heart and dropped it there.

"Lot thirty-seven," the auctioneer said. "Two weeks on Mr. Webster's private Caribbean island, known as Paradise. Do I hear a thousand?"

He did, and as he dropped into his patter, Kit tuned out the bidding and studied the audience. She saw Colette sitting very still, her lips pursed in what looked like disgust. Heather, beside her, was obviously trying to look sophisticated and bored. At a table not far from them, a young brunette almost bounced up and down in her eagerness to draw attention to her bids. On the opposite side of the stage was a gorgeous redhead who every now and then quietly raised a finger. And almost at center stage, squarely in front of the auctioneer, was a blonde who was almost studious about the whole thing, watching with interest and, whenever her turn came, raising a hand....

Susannah.

Susannah was bidding on Jarrett Webster.

Kit bolted from her seat at stage left and down the steps into the audience. Within thirty seconds she was beside Susannah, tugging at her upraised arm. "What are you *doing*, Sue?"

"I'm bidding," Susannah said calmly. "And don't look at me like that. You really can't get involved—how would it look?"

Kit gasped. "You're trying to buy him for me?"

"You don't think *I* want him, do you?"

As if drawn by a magnet, Kit's gaze slid to the stage, to Jarrett's face. He was looking straight at her, intently but without excitement—as if he had no real interest in what happened. Or, Kit thought grimly, as if he already knew the outcome. "Did he put you up to this?"

"Of course not." Susannah sounded shocked.

No, Kit thought. *He wouldn't have. A joke could only be carried so far before all the humor was gone....*

"Ali and I pooled our savings to pull it off. You've been working so hard, Kitty, and you need a break."

"That much is right. But I could use a break *from* Jarrett, not *with* him!"

Susannah had turned toward the stage. "Whose bid is it? I've lost track." She raised her hand anyway.

"I don't want him!"

Susannah looked her straight in the eyes and said gently, "Liar."

The single word dropped like a rock into a pool, and the ripples spread and crossed and amplified instead of receding.

"You're right," Kit whispered. She put her hand up, almost tentatively...

Just as the auctioneer said, "And gone...sold to the lady at stage right with the red hair. Congratulations, ma'am, and enjoy your trip!"

CHAPTER TEN

KIT DRAGGED her hand to her side. But she knew Jarrett
had seen that false move. In fact, despite the brightness
of the stage lights, she thought it was impossible for him
to have missed it—for where he was concerned, her luck
had never been any good.

And he no doubt found her embarrassment delightful.
Crazy, she told herself. *You've gone crazy.*

But at least the madness was past now. The hammer
had fallen, the auction was over, and there would be no
more temptation to make a fool of herself where Jarrett
was concerned. To that extent, at least, she was fortunate. Bidding on him would have been foolish enough.
But if she'd actually bought his dream date...

Two weeks in the Caribbean with Jarrett. Two weeks
of dreams come true. Followed, of course, by a lifetime
of regret.

As if, a rebellious little voice whispered in the back
of her mind, *you aren't going to have all the regrets,
anyway. At least you could have had some fun first.*

Jarrett came down the steps to the section of the ballroom reserved for the bachelors, and the stage was
empty save for the auctioneer. In the hush that followed,
Kit went straight to the podium to thank the auctioneer,
the bachelors, the bidders and the guests.

"I hope you've all enjoyed this evening," she finished, "whether you'll be going on a dream date or you
came tonight just for the fun of it. The auction is over,
but this isn't the end of the celebration. Please stay and

mingle, and take the opportunity to meet our generous bachelors.''

The ballroom lights came up, and a wave of applause swept the crowd. Kit, who would have liked to vanish into the back reaches of the hotel, once more descended the stairs from stage to ballroom floor, intending to greet and thank as many of the participants as she could.

The more adventurous of the bachelors had already swarmed out of the reserved section to seek out the women who had made the winning bids, and the more eager of the bidders pressed through the crowd to introduce themselves. The resulting confusion brought Kit to a standstill just outside the velvet ropes that blocked off the special section.

Jarrett was still in his chair, one elbow propped on a banquet table, fingertips pressed against his cheek in a thoughtful pose. Kit tried not to watch him, but she couldn't keep her gaze away.

He seemed to be staring into space. And he looked almost disheartened, she thought. Even unhappy...

Of course, she told herself briskly, it was a prize bit of wishful thinking to assume that because the man was sitting still in the midst of a mob, he must be miserable over the auction's outcome!

Determined to ignore him, she leaned across the velvet rope to start shaking hands, and she didn't see Jarrett move until he appeared beside her. ''You know,'' he said, ''if you're going to buy things at auctions you're going to have to learn to react a little faster, Kitten.''

''Who said I want to buy things at auctions?'' Kit smiled at a bidder and thanked her for coming.

''Correct me if I'm wrong,'' Jarrett said, ''but I would have sworn I saw your hand going up just as the hammer came down.''

''Oh, that. I knew your ego would be bruised if I

didn't bid at all, so I was going to put in just one offer to make you feel better.''

"What a shame it wasn't the winning bid. We could have had such a good time.'' His voice slowed, gentled. "All alone together, exploring a place called Paradise…''

Kit could feel the soft shivers of desire deep inside her. She shrugged with a casualness she was far from feeling. "Well, you'll still have two weeks of paradise. It just won't be me you're sharing it with—but I imagine you'll adjust, given a little time.''

"I really was hoping it would be you, Kitten.''

Kit's heart skipped a beat. Was he serious? He certainly sounded it.

Even if he was, she reminded herself, he was still obligated to the redhead who had bought him tonight. But if, after he came back, he still felt the same way… If he had discovered within himself the same kind of caring about Kit that she felt for him…

Her throat was suddenly tight with hope.

As if he'd seen the question in her eyes, Jarrett nodded. "Since you like the idea of roughing it, I was looking forward to telling you how the latest hurricane knocked out all the power and took the roof off the bungalow.''

I should just pick up a chair and hit him with it, Kit told herself. *Any jury in the world would understand!*

"Why am I not surprised?'' she said, and was proud of the wry note in her voice. "Of course, the lady who bought you might not be so pleased. After all, she paid a pretty penny for the privilege of spending two weeks with you, and she might like a roof thrown in.''

"Maybe,'' he said thoughtfully, "if you talk to her nicely, and tell her about the electricity and all, she'll sell the package to you.''

"You go right ahead and ask her. My offer stands—fourteen dollars, cash on the barrelhead."

"Don't forget the seventy-three cents," Jarrett said. "It might make a difference." He stepped over the velvet rope and strolled off across the ballroom, in no apparent hurry.

Kit shook her head and turned to a knot of bachelors, the last ones remaining in the reserved section. "Of course there's still the main event to get through," one of them said. "And I thought ordinary blind dates were a nightmare."

"Oh, I don't know," the man next to him remarked. "It wasn't so bad, after all. I'm almost glad Webster twisted my arm."

A bystander punched him lightly in the shoulder. "What are you complaining about? I saw the women who were bidding on you. Now *I* have a reason to fuss. He practically blackmailed me, and the next time I see Jarrett I'm going to tell him—"

Kit didn't hear the rest, for a few simple words were echoing in her brain. *Twisted my arm. Blackmail. Jarrett...*

Her head was spinning. He hadn't trusted her to bring this off after all—so he hadn't given her a chance.

He had challenged her to raise ten thousand dollars and threatened to destroy her business and her partners if she didn't succeed. But all the time, while he'd been ostensibly holding back and giving her the opportunity to prove herself, he had been working behind the scenes—not to ruin her plans, as she'd feared for so long, but to make the auction successful.

No wonder Tryad's phones had rung off the wall with eager bachelors demanding to be included—Jarrett had forced them to volunteer. No wonder the tickets had almost sold out—Jarrett had probably arranged that, too.

He, not Kit, was almost singlehandedly responsible for tonight's success.

But the effect on Kit was precisely the same as if he'd carried out the sabotage she'd feared—for by taking over, he had robbed her of her accomplishment and credibility. She hadn't proved a thing, because he hadn't allowed her the chance to show her capabilities.

And all the while, as Kit had congratulated herself on her success, he'd no doubt been laughing at her shortsightedness, at the ego that had let her believe she alone was responsible.

"Kitten," he said behind her. "I'd like you to meet Nancy. I told her you were having regrets about not buying me, but I'm afraid she doesn't seem eager to negotiate."

Kit didn't even glance at the redhead on his arm. "You set me up," she snapped.

Jarrett's eyebrows rose. "I beg your pardon?"

"You didn't play fair, Jarrett. You didn't let me have a chance to show what I can do."

"If you could be just a bit more specific, Kitten—"

"We're talking about your *help*. Perhaps I ought to be grateful for everything you did, Jarrett, but I'm not. If you'd been open about it—sincere—I'd have been delighted to have assistance. But you couldn't just help, could you? No—you went behind my back, fixing things up without telling me, interfering in everything…" She stumbled on, her voice choked with tears. "Why did you do it, Jarrett? So you could feel sanctimonious about destroying Tryad, after all, and still do a good turn for a wonderful cause?"

"Kitten—"

"Don't ever call me that again. In fact, don't ever come near me again." She shot a look at the redhead, who was just as gorgeous in full light as she'd been in the dimness of the ballroom. "Congratulations, Nancy," she went on briskly. "I hope you have a great time in the Caribbean. And I'm glad you don't want to make a deal—because I'd rather spend a year in prison than two weeks in Paradise with him!"

The final tally was better than Kit had hoped for, even in her wildest flights of fancy. After all the bills were paid, the auction would net several times her original pledge. In fact, it was an astounding success by any standards—and for a fund-raiser that had been created from scratch in less than three weeks, it was incredible.

Under other circumstances, Kit told herself glumly, she'd have been very proud.

"It's not only a feather in Tryad's cap," Susannah said at breakfast on Monday morning, when she heard Kit's report of the bottom line, "but you're now our acknowledged champion when it comes to fund drives."

"If that means you're going to try to shuffle your money-raising problems off on me, Sue—"

Susannah had gone straight on. "Though I wonder... Are you absolutely certain you wouldn't rather have lost the bet and slept with him?"

Alison's gaze slid from Kit's face to her untouched English muffin, and she briskly told Susannah to shut up.

For a moment, Kit thought Alison was going to reach across the table and give her a comforting hug.

Instead Alison said, "Well, at least with that finally over, we can get back to regular business." She shuffled papers for a moment. "And there's plenty of it to do. Industrial Dynamics has been sued because of a conveyer belt they produced, and the CEO wants a plan to head off trouble from other customers who have bought the same types of belts." Her tone was all business.

Kit was grateful. The last thing she needed was sympathy. Loaded onto her fragile pride, it might well be the straw that would break her. But given a little time to heal...

She was already a bit calmer, now that thirty-six hours had passed—though she was no less hurt. And she had no regrets about what she'd said to Jarrett, either. Helping was one thing. The job had been big enough for everyone, and she'd have gratefully accepted his assistance. But interfering, as he'd done, was something else.

She hoped that with time the pain would recede and more pleasant memories would move to the foreground. And there *were* plenty of pleasant memories. The basketball game and the visit to Milady Lingerie, the banter and the chats, the kisses...

She would hang onto those things, for there was nothing else to cling to.

Kit's office was chaotic, with papers stacked and loose ends waiting to be tied up. She tidied her desk enough to make room to work and found a dart under a stack of folders. Automatically, she turned to throw it at the board across the room. But Jarrett's portrait was smiling at her from the dartboard, and she found she couldn't aim it at him, after all.

She walked across the office. The last dart she'd thrown at him was still stuck in the portrait, squarely over his heart.

If only it had been as easy to touch the real one.

Kit pulled the dart out carefully and unpinned the picture from the board. While there were pinholes here and there where the needle-sharp darts had punctured it, the photo wasn't as badly damaged as she'd expected. She hadn't had much time in the last few days to take out her frustrations on anything.

She laid the picture on her desk blotter and smoothed its wounds, using her thumbnail to press each pinhole closed. She couldn't conceal them entirely, of course, but now it took a closer inspection to spot them.

Tucking the photograph in a manila folder, she filed it in her desk drawer. Maybe someday she'd be strong enough to put the hurt behind her altogether and remember only the humor. Eventually, perhaps, she'd frame it. Not that she'd need the reminder—she would never forget Jarrett, or anything about him. But it would be nice to look up from her work and see him there.

Cut it out, Deevers, she told herself, *or the next thing you know, you'll be sobbing.*

She picked up the telephone before she could talk herself out of it and dialed his private number. When a woman answered, Kit was disappointed. She had so much wanted, one last time, to feel his voice, rich and warm as a soft blanket surrounding and comforting her.

Of course, she reminded herself, he was far more apt to be curt and cool than warm and welcoming. If he'd been in any mood to apologize—or even to explain— he'd had all day Sunday to call her and do so. The fact that he'd remained completely silent didn't show much promise.

"This is Kit Deevers, calling for Mr. Webster," she said.

The secretary's voice was calmly professional. "I'm afraid Mr. Webster isn't available at the moment."

Kit wondered if that meant he was unavailable only to her. She wouldn't be surprised. On the other hand, she told herself, she probably wasn't important enough for him to go to any great lengths to avoid her. "In the next few days, I'll be writing a check for the funds we raised with the Dream Dates Auction last weekend, and I'm calling to ask how the payee should be listed."

"I'll certainly give him the message as soon as possible."

She gave no hint of when that might be, Kit noted. Had Nancy been so eager to cash in her two weeks in the Caribbean that they'd already left?

"You might also ask if he'd like me to mail the check to him so he can present it, or directly to the charity." That, Kit thought, would make it clear—in the unlikely event she hadn't gotten her point across in the ballroom Saturday night—that she wasn't expecting to see him again.

With everything possible done for the moment, she put the dream dates file aside and turned to the new project Alison had detailed over breakfast. There was no doubt the company's conveyer belt had caused injury to a worker, but someone at the injured man's work site had circumvented at least three built-in safety measures that would have prevented the injury. The touchy question, Kit decided, was how to get that across to the public, particularly Industrial Dynamics' other customers, without appearing to bad-mouth the one who'd had the problem.

With relief, Kit plunged into work, and hours later when the telephone on her desk rang she looked at it almost blankly for an instant with her mind still on conveyer belts before thinking, *It's Jarrett....*

Her heart was skipping like an Irish jig as she picked up the phone. It wasn't that she expected this conversation to make any real difference, she told herself firmly. Still, Jarrett might have had a change of heart.

But it wasn't Jarrett, only Rita, and Kit's heart settled sadly into place, a leaden lump in the center of her chest.

"You've been so absorbed all day that I thought I'd better call to remind you," the secretary said.

"Of what?"

"You have an appointment with the child abuse hot line people this afternoon."

Kit drew a sharp breath. "To deliver the finished campaign for their new phone number. You're a darling, Rita. I'd have forgotten it for sure."

"It's at four o'clock," Rita added, "so I'll probably be gone by the time you get back. That's the other reason I'm bothering you now. There's a message for you from Mr. Webster."

A message? She'd told Rita to screen her calls today, as all three of them did when an important project loomed. But she had no doubt Jarrett was capable of charming Rita and getting through her most determined objections. Or hadn't he asked to speak to Kit?

"It's just the name of a domestic violence organization," Rita said. "The secretary said you'd know what it meant."

A secretary. He hadn't called himself. The last bit of feeble hope in Kit's heart crumbled into dust.

She was a fool, she told herself curtly, to hope that she might be important enough to him to rate an apology—or even an explanation.

That is the end of that, she thought. At least now she could face the future, because she knew for certain there was no reason to look back.

The people at the child abuse hot line service hadn't seen the media campaign she'd created for them, and they were duly impressed by the finished product. Kit explained the process, answered questions, gave advice and received compliments—though she wasn't quite sure what she was saying. Despite the warm reception, by the time she left, she felt almost as if she were escaping.

The business day was done. Of course, there was plenty of work waiting in her office—but she was hardly in a frame of mind to accomplish much, and there was no point in putting in hours. Better to start fresh in the morning.

Which left the problem of what to do with herself tonight. Sit at home and think about evenings just past—evenings spent with Jarrett? Not a good option. But going out somewhere was no guarantee she wouldn't still be thinking of him.

Her key ring had slid clear to the bottom of her handbag, and she practically had to dump the contents of the bag on the hood of her car before she could find her car key. Obviously, it was time to clean out the mess. She couldn't believe the amount of junk that had collected in the bag in a matter of weeks.

Well, that would entertain her for part of the evening, she thought dryly—even though, as an excuse for staying home, it was on a par with washing her hair.

She picked up a tiny beige brocade makeup bag and debated for a moment whether she should put it in her purse or dump it in the nearby garbage can. She hadn't opened it since the barely clad model had thrust it into her hands at Milady Lingerie.

It seemed so long ago, she thought wistfully. That evening, Jarrett had treated her as if she was really a part of his world, and—though she hadn't yet realized how she felt about him—she'd responded like a woman in love.

She held the bag over the garbage can for a long moment. Then, her fingers trembling, she slipped it into the pocket of her blazer.

She knew it was silly to imagine that going to the store might help her recapture the glorious glow she'd felt when she was with him. But her body seemed suddenly to have a mind of its own, and instead of driving toward the lake and home, she turned toward the sub-urbs.

The front view of Milady Lingerie was still a treat to the eye, even though some of the romantic atmosphere was diluted by the sunshine that streamed through sky-lights in the mall's main walkway.

Or perhaps, Kit admitted, it only seemed less romantic because today she was alone.

There were other changes, too. No marchers were car-rying signs. Jarrett's policy of making no fuss seemed to have discouraged them faster than any amount of legal action could have.

I could have told them they needed public relations advice, she thought.

The red teddy was gone from the window, and a lavender silk dressing gown, trimmed in what looked like antique tatting, had taken its place. Kit wondered if the new magazine ads were already on the stands or if the store's manager had jumped the gun a bit.

She fingered the satin bag in her pocket for courage and went in.

There was no one in sight. Not a customer, not a clerk. And since there was no merchandise within view, either, Kit couldn't help but wonder how on earth Milady Lingerie turned a profit. How did a prospective customer decide what she wanted to buy? Or know what to ask for?

A young woman came from the back of the store. "Hello. What can I help you with today?"

"I don't..." Kit almost stammered. She glanced to-ward the door. "I've got a gift certificate, but I'm not sure—"

"So at the moment you're just looking?" The woman smiled. "Aren't we all? Come to the fitting rooms and we'll measure you first. Then we can really have fun selecting the things that will flatter you most."

Before Kit could demur, she found herself standing in a fitting room in nothing but her underwear. While the fitter worked, Kit looked around in surprise. With its velvet fainting couch and the watercolor on the wall, the room looked more like a boudoir than the utilitarian dressing nooks most stores provided.

"You have lovely posture," the fitter murmured. "That straight back will carry off almost anything we stock."

"I've been told my shoulder blades are my best feature," Kit said dryly.

"Well, it's not a bad thing. Unlike some pretty faces, shoulder blades last forever. And as for your coloring, you'll look wonderful in peach and ivory and teal... Let me go and get a few things for you to look at."

She brought silky underthings and lacy nightwear, satin slippers and a bathrobe as light and delicate as gossamer. And after they were tried on and exclaimed over, she went after another load.

Before long, silk and satin and lace were not only piled high on the fainting couch but had spilled onto the carpet, and Kit was revising her opinions of the way Jarrett ran his business.

Everything was lovely. Everything was just the right shade to flatter her. Everything was a perfect fit. And Kit had no idea how she could possibly choose an item or two from among the beauty strewn around her.

Which, from Jarrett's perspective, must be the whole point. If every woman who walked into Milady Lingerie reacted like this...

"I really can't buy all of this," Kit said helplessly. Even to herself, she didn't sound convincing.

The fitter laughed. "Heavens, *nobody* can buy everything she looks good in. But we'll make a list of what you like best, and then on your birthday or Christmas, your significant other can come in and do his shopping the easy way. And he'll get the right size, too—which, if he's anything like my husband, makes a pleasant change.''

Except, Kit thought, *my significant other won't be shopping for me.* The lump in her throat threatened to choke her.

She picked up a dainty confection in cream-colored silk and lace, with satin ribbons and delicate embroidery. Of all the lovely things the fitter had brought, this was the closest to the white lace outfit Jarrett had supposedly designed especially for her. Or perhaps he would have settled on black velvet, after all. She would never know.

"I'll take this," she said. Her voice was almost gruff.

She handed over not only the gift certificate but her credit card to cover the balance, and picked up her bag—heavy, satiny paper in the same neutral beige as the furnishings in the drawing room.

It was a foolish purchase, Kit knew. She wasn't sure what the garment was called, and she would probably never wear it. But she'd keep it forever.

She stepped into the drawing room, bag in hand, and froze as Jarrett, sitting on the love seat before the fireplace, looked up from a magazine and got lazily to his feet. "Hello," he said. "Did you find something you like?"

The drawing room was spacious. It was impossible that he was physically blocking her from reaching the doorway. All she had to do, Kit knew, was walk past him and into the mall. But her feet seemed to be glued to the carpet.

Where the words came from, she didn't know. "It'll

do. I always think it's such a shame to waste a gift certificate.''

"I don't suppose you'd consider modeling your purchase for me? Because of the gift certificate, in a sense I paid for it, so it would be only fair if—''

"You can certainly afford it. And remember? I told you a long time ago I wouldn't be caught dead modeling for you.''

"In the magazine ads, no. I'd already thought better of that. But I thought perhaps in real life—''

She faced him squarely. "If you hope this kind of talk is going to get you off the hook, Jarrett, forget it. Why did you pull strings? And why did you do it all behind the scenes? So you could still go around Chicago telling tales about Tryad?" Her voice cracked. "About how I took the credit for a success that wasn't mine at all—''

"Is that why you're so upset, Kit? Not that I did those things, but because I didn't tell you I was doing them?''

"Give the man an award for sensitivity,'' Kit snapped. "You deliberately led me into embarrassing myself, and now—''

"No, Kit.'' His voice was almost gentle. "There was nothing deliberate about it. And the only one who seems to be worried about the possibility of you being embarrassed is you.''

Kit's hands clenched on the back of a wing chair. She was vaguely surprised that her nails didn't cut the brocade upholstery. "You—''

"I'd hoped that after a couple of days to think it over, perhaps you'd calm down enough to listen to my side of it,'' he said. "But if not—''

"You may as well go ahead,'' Kit said reluctantly. "I've got nothing to lose by hearing what you have to say.''

He looked at her for a long moment as if debating,

then sat on the arm of the love seat. "I was furious about the mess that fashion show turned into. It was a waste of time and resources."

Kit couldn't argue with that. She nodded stiffly.

"It wasn't the fault of the people who contributed to it that their money hadn't done any good. But they'd made a donation in good faith, so it was impossible to go back and ask for more because what they'd already given was wasted. So a good cause was cheated—"

"And you thought I was the one doing the cheating."

"It certainly looked bad for you, especially since everyone connected with the fashion show told me the same things about what had happened."

"People like Colette and Heather," Kit said bitterly, "who eagerly blamed all the problems on me."

"Exactly. They're the reason I decided to check you out."

Kit was startled. "They... But I don't understand."

"I've learned, over the years, to believe about ten percent of what those two females tell me. The trouble sometimes is knowing exactly which ten percent is the truth. So I went to Tryad to check you out myself. Were you the cold and scheming sort who'd steal from a desperate cause? Or had you gotten stuck in circumstances?" He added thoughtfully, "You greeted me very ungraciously that afternoon, if you recall."

Kit remembered, all right—she'd been nervous and defensive, on edge and wary. "I didn't even ask you to sit down."

"That's right. You were a very cool customer. The kind, I thought, who wouldn't care much about any cause, especially if it got in the way of your profits. So, in anger, I gave you a challenge. If you succeeded, you would at least make up for the mess the fashion show had turned into. But if you tried to pull a single stunt—"

"Then you'd have good cause to ruin me."

"Better than Colette's and Heather's opinions, that's sure."

"Well," Kit mused, "I suppose it's some comfort that at least you didn't condemn me on their word."

"I gave you my ultimatum. And then you did two things that were really strange."

"Only two?" Kit's list would have been a whole lot longer than that.

"You didn't seem concerned about yourself but about your partners—and somehow that didn't sound like the hard, cold woman I thought I was seeing. And then you pulled off that press conference to announce the auction and really threw down the gauntlet—and I was fascinated. You'd taken on a tremendous job, more than I'd even dreamed of asking."

"Too bad you didn't tell me I didn't have to go to such lengths."

He smiled. "It was too late for that—you'd made sure of it. I still didn't know, though, quite *why* you were doing it. Was it my threat or your own nature that was making you work so hard? And I kept reminding myself that just because you weren't pulling any obvious tricks this time didn't mean you weren't capable of it."

"So you watched."

"And I started quietly pulling a few strings."

"For the sake of the cause?" Kit asked, almost bitterly. "Or to make sure there was enough money that it would be worth my while to steal some of it?"

"At first, maybe. But by the end, I did it because I wanted you to succeed."

"You should have told me what you were doing."

He nodded. "You're no doubt right, but I thought it didn't make any difference. You'd never know that I had anything to do with it, and your glorious success would give you and Tryad a boost. It would help make up for my doubt and the threats I'd made.''

She thought it over. ''Why?'' she asked finally. The word was little more than a whisper.

''You're a puzzle, Kit. An enigma. I wanted to stick around till I could figure out which was the real you—the efficient and cool lady who had everything under control or the scatterbrained, hodgepodge female who couldn't even put her clothes on right.''

''Don't tease me about that,'' she said softly. ''I never pretended to be any competition for the Lingerie Ladies.''

His gaze drifted over her from head to foot. ''Don't you know,'' he asked soberly, ''that you are shatteringly lovely, and that you always will be?''

Kit gulped. She didn't dare let herself take him seriously. All she could do was try to make a joke of it. ''If you make one more remark about my shoulder blades, Jarrett Webster—''

''Oh, there are women who have more perfect shapes than you, and women whose faces are technically more beautiful. But you are an original, Kit, and part of your attraction is the fact that you are uncertain of your charm and unaware that you are special.'' His voice dropped even lower. ''And you are very, very desirable.''

The mere word was enough to set off a reaction that rocked Kit to the core. Longing flickered through her veins like fire consuming living grass, slowly, sensually, irrevocably.

''And yet,'' Jarrett said, ''sometimes you weren't uncertain at all. You knew exactly what you thought of me. You were putting up with me, no more. Whenever I made any move toward getting serious—''

Kit frowned. If he was talking about all the times he'd

suggested they have an affair—well, that was hardly what she'd call serious.

"You'd back away or turn it into a joke. I mentioned the Riviera, and you suggested an army tent in Iceland."

"You *meant* that?" she whispered.

"When I offered you two weeks in the Caribbean—two weeks that could truly have been paradise—you shrugged it off as if you didn't care."

There was no denying the pain in his voice, and Kit could feel herself healing as he spoke. She didn't know if he would ever call what he felt for her *love*—but she didn't care. The emotion, not the name, was what counted, and she knew that he, too, felt this tie between them.

"I cared," she said huskily. "I cared too much."

The words were like a pebble dropped into a still pond. It took a moment for the ripples to appear, but once started, they would go on forever.

Jarrett's hands cupped her face, and for a long moment he stared into her eyes. Then with a little groan he caught her close. His kiss was fire, welding her heart to his, and Kit wanted it never to end. Everything was all right, now that they were together.

Except...

Eventually, she drew away from him. "You still have to take Nancy to the Caribbean," she reminded him.

Jarrett sighed. "Yes, that is a bit of a complication. Do you mind?"

"Yes."

"Good." He smiled at her, and his arms tightened. "I love you, Kit."

Kit thought she was going to explode with happiness. "I love you, too," she whispered, and once more his mouth took hers.

When she could breathe again, she asked, "Did you just wander into the store this afternoon?"

Jarrett relaxed his hold a fraction and complained, "Kitten, you have a very inconvenient habit of letting your mind wander when I'm doing my best to kiss you senseless."

"Then it's obvious you'll have to practice."

He smiled and drew her closer once more. "My pleasure."

Kit put both hands on his chest. "But in the meantime, you haven't answered my question. Did you just happen to come in?"

"Of course not. The manager called to tell me you were here."

"Really? Does she personally report all customers or just ones who have been spotted with you on previous occasions?"

"She thought I might be especially interested in this case, so she arranged for you to look at everything in the store till I got here."

"I'm disappointed if that means not every customer gets the sort of attention and service I did."

"We do the best we can in that regard, but I'd say you got the VIP treatment." He released her and stepped to the door, beckoning to someone in the back room. "That reminds me—I'd like to formally introduce you. Kitten, you do remember Nancy?"

The gorgeous redhead came into the drawing room, and Jarrett slipped an arm around her shoulders.

Kit gasped. "Nancy's the manager of this place?"

"And she's my sister," Jarrett said.

Nancy smiled—it was very like Jarrett's smile—and held out a hand. "Spending two weeks on the island would be fine," she said. "But there's no way I want this guy taking up space next to *my* deck chair, so I'm glad you've worked it out.''

Kit's head was spinning. She'd suspected that the story of a home in Europe might be a cover-up. But she'd never have expected Jarrett's sister to work for him. And yet, what a perfect hiding place it would be. And she could understand why Nancy had chosen it, as well, for there was pride in her face and in the way she stood. She wasn't a woman who could be offered a handout, that was certain. It was incredible for a woman who had been battered to have brought her self-esteem to such a level.

''She's fantastic,'' she said, after Nancy had gone to her office.

''In lots of ways.'' He tipped his head as he looked at Kit. ''Including braving her fears of being spotted by Chicago society just to buy me. You don't think I'd have left something so important to chance, do you?''

''No. But Susannah was bidding, too, and I thought—''

''That I'd set her up to do it? Oh, no. She's too good a friend of yours, and I knew if you told her to cut it out, she would. And of course she did.''

''But wait a minute. Then who's Colette? You said something about family when Heather offered to rig the auction, so I thought *she* might be your sister.''

''Second cousin. Unfortunately, that's not quite close enough for me to turn her daughter over my knee.''

''Too bad.''

''Isn't it, though? We'll have to talk about Heather sometime. But just now we have far more interesting things to think about.''

''Yes.'' Kit's voice trailed off, and then with sudden firmness she said, ''I have a confession to make, Jarrett. I didn't expect you to cooperate with the auction.''

Jarrett shook his head chidingly. "That was foolish of you. By then I was far too intrigued not to." He settled her more comfortably in his arms and gently rested his chin against her hair. "I think the reason I was so angry in the first place was because I was attracted to you from the very beginning."

"Must have been the harem outfit."

"That didn't hurt. Then I thought for a while that an affair would do it, that I could get you out of my system that way. Now I know it'll take a lifelong affair. So—" He tipped her face up to his. "Marry me, Kit?"

"Are you serious?"

"Never more so. There's nothing I won't do for a good cause—even get married."

Kit frowned.

He went on happily. "Just think—a wedding coming out of this year's auction will make an enormous splash to promote the next one."

"You mean there's going to be another one?"

"Why not? It was a great show. And next year we can play up the romance angle."

"*You* won't be available."

"True. But perhaps it will happen to someone else. And as long as they have the dream of finding happiness like this…" He kissed her once more, a long and lingering caress that set Kit's nerves aflame. She ran her fingers through his hair, exulting in the freedom to touch him.

"No," he said. His voice was a little shaky. "*Definitely* you're no competition for the Lingerie Ladies. They can't begin to measure up."

"Are you certain you're not just besotted?"

"Maybe—but if so, I don't expect to get over it. And when you wear white lace, it's going to be just for me,

on our wedding night. How about it, Kitten? Will you
be my very own personal Lingerie Lady—forever?''

Kit smiled slowly at him and drew his lips to hers.

* * * * *

Look out next month for Susannah's story in
THE PLAYBOY ASSIGNMENT

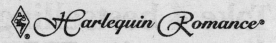

Harlequin Romance®

is delighted to bring you
a brilliant new trilogy
from bestselling author

Leigh
Michaels

Finding *Mr Right*

**Three women definitely *not* looking for
love—but it finds them anyway!**

Kit, Susannah and Alison are best friends and partners.
Successful and happily single, they're busy running their own
business and have no intention of looking for husbands...
until each finds a man they simply can't resist!

Find your Mr Right, starting in March:

March 1998—THE BILLIONAIRE DATE (#3496)
April 1998—THE PLAYBOY ASSIGNMENT (#3500)
May 1998—THE HUSBAND PROJECT (#3504)

Available in March, April and May,
wherever Harlequin books are sold.

Take 4 bestselling love stories FREE

Plus get a FREE surprise gift!

Special Limited-time Offer

Mail to Harlequin Reader Service®

P.O. Box 609
Fort Erie, Ontario
L2A 5X3

YES! Please send me 4 free Harlequin Romance® novels and my free surprise gift. Then send me 6 brand-new novels every month, which I will receive months before they appear in bookstores. Bill me at the low price of $3.34 each plus 25¢ delivery and GST*. That's the complete price and a savings of over 10% off the cover prices—quite a bargain! I understand that accepting the books and gift places me under no obligation ever to buy any books. I can always return a shipment and cancel at any time. Even if I never buy another book from Harlequin, the 4 free books and the surprise gift are mine to keep forever.

316 HEN CE64

Name	(PLEASE PRINT)	
Address		Apt. No.
City	Province	Postal Code

This offer is limited to one order per household and not valid to present Harlequin Romance® subscribers. *Terms and prices are subject to change without notice. Canadian residents will be charged applicable provincial taxes and GST.

CROM-696   ©1990 Harlequin Enterprises Limited

DEBBIE MACOMBER

invites you to the

HEART OF TEXAS

Join Debbie Macomber as she brings you the lives and loves of the folks in the ranching community of Promise, Texas.

If you loved Midnight Sons—don't miss Heart of Texas! A brand-new six-book series from Debbie Macomber.

Available in February 1998 at your favorite retail store.

Heart of Texas by Debbie Macomber

Lonesome Cowboy	February '98
Texas Two-Step	March '98
Caroline's Child	April '98
Dr. Texas	May '98
Nell's Cowboy	June '98
Lone Star Baby	July '98

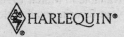

HARLEQUIN®

HPHRT1

BESTSELLING AUTHORS
IN THE SPOTLIGHT

.WE'RE SHINING THE SPOTLIGHT ON SIX OF OUR STARS!

Harlequin and Silhouette have selected stories from several of their bestselling authors to give you six sensational reads. These star-powered romances are bound to please!

THERE'S A PRICE TO PAY FOR STARDOM... AND IT'S LOW

$1.99 U.S. $2.50 CAN. Special Offer

As a special offer, these six outstanding books are available from Harlequin and Silhouette for only $1.99 in the U.S. and $2.50 in Canada. Watch for these titles:

At the Midnight Hour—**Alicia Scott**
Joshua and the Cowgirl—**Sherryl Woods**
Another Whirlwind Courtship—**Barbara Boswell**
✓*Madeleine's Cowboy*—**Kristine Rolofson**
Her Sister's Baby—**Janice Kay Johnson**
One and One Makes Three—**Muriel Jensen**

Available in March 1998
at your favorite retail outlet.

PBAIS

Welcome to *Love Inspired*™

A brand-new series of contemporary inspirational love stories.

Join men and women as they learn valuable lessons about facing the challenges of today's world and about life, love and faith.

**Look for the following March 1998
Love Inspired™ titles:**

CHILD OF HER HEART
by Irene Brand

A FATHER'S LOVE
by Cheryl Wolverton

WITH BABY IN MIND
by Arlene James

Available in retail outlets in February 1998.

LIFT YOUR SPIRITS AND GLADDEN YOUR HEART
with *Love Inspired!*™

Steeple
Hill™

LI398

HARLEQUIN ULTIMATE GUIDES™

A series of how-to books for today's woman.

Act now to order some of these extremely
helpful guides just for you!

*Whatever the situation, Harlequin Ultimate Guides™
has all the answers!*

#80507	HOW TO TALK TO A	$4.99 U.S.	☐
	NAKED MAN	$5.50 CAN.	☐
#80508	I CAN FIX THAT	$5.99 U.S.	☐
		$6.99 CAN.	☐
#80510	WHAT YOUR TRAVEL AGENT	$5.99 U.S.	☐
	KNOWS THAT YOU DON'T	$6.99 CAN.	☐
#80511	RISING TO THE OCCASION		
	More Than Manners: Real Life	$5.99 U.S.	☐
	Etiquette for Today's Woman	$6.99 CAN.	☐
#80513	WHAT GREAT CHEFS	$5.99 U.S.	☐
	KNOW THAT YOU DON'T	$6.99 CAN.	☐
#80514	WHAT SAVVY INVESTORS	$5.99 U.S.	☐
	KNOW THAT YOU DON'T	$6.99 CAN.	☐
#80509	GET WHAT YOU WANT OUT OF	$5.99 U.S.	☐
	LIFE—AND KEEP IT!	$6.99 CAN.	☐

(quantities may be limited on some titles)

TOTAL AMOUNT	$
POSTAGE & HANDLING	$
($1.00 for one book, 50¢ for each additional)	
APPLICABLE TAXES*	$ _____
TOTAL PAYABLE	$ _____
(check or money order—please do not send cash)	

To order, complete this form and send it, along with a check or money
order for the total above, payable to Harlequin Ultimate Guides, to:
In the U.S.: 3010 Walden Avenue, P.O. Box 9047, Buffalo, NY
14269-9047; **In Canada:** P.O. Box 613, Fort Erie, Ontario, L2A 5X3.

Name: _____

Address: _____ City: _____

State/Prov.: _____ Zip/Postal Code: _____

*New York residents remit applicable sales taxes.
Canadian residents remit applicable GST and provincial taxes.

HARLEQUIN®